The Orphaɪ Mi

©2024 by Molly Britton

Contents

Chapter One

Mary's father was never around.

Each day, she sat by the small window, eyes wide with worry, counting the hours until his return. Some nights, he didn't come back at all, leaving her shivering in the darkness, her belly empty and her mind filled with dread. When he did stumble home, he reeked of strange smells and collapsed into bed, his slurred mumblings leaving her confused and scared. At just ten years old, Mary didn't understand why her father was like this.

All she knew was that he was all she had left since her mother had died three years ago giving birth to her baby brother, who hadn't survived either.

Mary stared out of the grimy window, her eyes fixed on the bustling docks below. The room she and her father shared was meagre, containing a single bed, a rickety table, and a couple of creaky chairs. The thin walls barely kept out the sounds of the busy street and the constant din from the other tenants. Clutching her mother's old shawl around her shoulders, Mary found a small measure of comfort in its faded, familiar fabric.

One evening, as Mary waited anxiously for her father's return, she heard laughter outside. Pressing her nose against the cold glass, she saw a group of children playing a game of tag. Their laughter echoed through the narrow alley, a stark contrast to her own lonely existence. She longed to join them, to feel the joy they seemed to take for granted, but fear held her back. Instead, she retreated to the bed, pulling the thin covers over her head.

"One day, maybe," she whispered to herself, her voice lost in the silence of the room.

Days turned into weeks, and Mary's routine remained unchanged. Her father left early each morning and returned late at night, often smelling of alcohol. On the rare occasions when he was sober, he was distant, lost in his own grief. Mary missed the warmth and love she once felt from her parents. She often thought of the time when her family was whole, and life was filled with laughter and joy.

One particularly cold and rainy night, her father did not return at all. Mary waited by the window, her small frame shivering from the damp chill. As the hours dragged on, fear gripped her heart. She imagined the worst, her mind conjuring up terrible scenarios of what might have happened to him. Eventually, exhaustion overcame her, and she fell asleep by the window, tears staining her cheeks.

The next morning, Mary was awakened by the creak of the door. Her father stumbled in, drenched and dishevelled. He collapsed onto the bed, mumbling incoherently. Mary approached him cautiously, her heart aching for the man who was both her protector and the cause of her sorrow. She gently covered him with a blanket, her small hands trembling.

"Daddy," she whispered, "are you all right?"

He groaned in response, his eyes barely open. "Just tired, Mary. Go back to sleep."

As she sat beside him, watching him sleep, Mary vowed to be strong. She knew she had to take care of herself and her father, even if he was not always there for her.

***

The following day, her father took her to a large building constructed of bricks stained with soot. It was big and imposing, surrounded by a towering metal fence. Mary looked up at the imposing structure, her small hand gripping her father's calloused one tightly.

"Daddy, what is this place? Why are we here?" she asked, her voice trembling.

He glanced down at her, his eyes shadowed with sorrow and something else she couldn't quite understand. "It's an orphanage, Mary. You'll be living here from now on."

As they walked through the iron gates and up the stone steps, Mary's heart sank. She had heard of orphanages, places where children without parents went to live. Her father's words echoed in her ears, and she felt a surge of panic.

"No, Daddy, please! Take me home!" she cried, tears streaming down her face.

Her father didn't meet her gaze. He simply led her inside, his grip on her hand firm but distant. The inside of the orphanage was dim and cold, with stone floors that echoed their footsteps and high ceilings that seemed to press down on Mary. The air smelled faintly of disinfectant and something musty, like old books.

They walked past rows of wooden benches and long tables where children sat, their faces pale and expressionless. Some glanced up at Mary with curiosity, others with a kind of resigned sadness. She clung to her father's hand, her tears falling freely now.

"Please, Daddy, don't leave me here," she sobbed, but he kept walking, his face a mask of resolve.

They reached a door at the end of a long corridor. Her father knocked, and a stern voice from within bid them to enter. Inside was a study, lined with shelves filled with dusty tomes and ledgers. A large, heavy desk dominated the room, and behind it sat an elderly woman with sharp eyes and a severe expression. Her grey hair was pulled back into a tight bun, and she wore a dark, formal dress that seemed as old as the building itself.

"Good afternoon, sir," the woman said, her voice brisk and businesslike. "This must be Mary."

Mary's father nodded, his eyes fixed on a spot on the floor. "Yes, Mrs Hemmings. This is Mary. She... she needs a place to stay."

Mrs Hemmings rose from her chair and walked around the desk, her eyes appraising

Mary with a critical gaze. "Very well," she said, her tone softening slightly. "We will take good care of her."

Mary felt her father's hand slip from hers as he stepped back. She reached out, trying to grab hold of him, but he moved away too quickly. "Daddy, please!" she cried, her voice breaking.

He finally looked at her, his expression blank. "You'll be fine here, Mary."

"There, there, child," Mrs Hemmings said, not unkindly. "Stop your crying at once. Tears solve nothing."

Mary's father hesitated at the door, his back to them. "Look after her, Mrs Hemmings," he said, his voice wavering. "She's a good girl."

Mrs Hemmings narrowed her eyes at Mary. "A good girl, you say? Then why are you leaving her here? Must have done something to warrant this."

Mary's father turned to face them, his eyes blank. He said nothing, and Mary felt fear bubble up in her chest as they locked eyes.

Mrs Hemmings sniffed, her expression stern. "Well, whatever the case, she'll learn discipline here. We don't tolerate nonsense."

Mary's sobs grew louder, and she reached out to her father. "Daddy, please don't leave me!"

Her father stepped forward, kneeling to her level. He took her hands in his, his grip trembling. "You listen to Mrs Hemmings. Do what she says now, and you'll be just fine."

Mrs Hemmings crossed her arms, her eyes hard. "Enough of this sentimental drivel. The girl needs to learn her place. We'll whip her into shape."

Mary's father stood slowly, nodding. "Good."

Mrs Hemmings gave a curt nod. "She'll get what she needs."

With a final glance at Mary, her father turned and walked out of the room. The door closed behind him, the sound final and crushing.

Mary's legs gave way, and she collapsed onto the floor, crying uncontrollably. Mrs Hemmings loomed over her, her expression cold and unyielding.

"Get up, child," she commanded. "There's no place for weakness here. You must learn to be strong."

Mary looked up at her, her eyes pleading. "I didn't do anything wrong. Please, let me go home."

Mrs Hemmings shook her head, her lips pressed into a thin line. "Your father brought you here, and here you shall stay. We'll see to it that you behave properly."

As Mrs Hemmings led Mary away, the reality of her new life began to sink in. The walls seemed to close in around her, and the echoes of her father's footsteps faded into the oppressive silence of the orphanage.

Chapter Two

Mrs Hemmings took Mary by the hand and led her down a long, dimly lit corridor. The walls were bare, and the air felt damp and cold. Mary tried to stifle her sobs, but they came out in small, hiccupping gasps.

"Enough of that now," Mrs Hemmings said sharply. "Crying won't help you here."

They stopped in front of a heavy wooden door, which Mrs Hemmings pushed open to reveal a large, overcrowded room. The room was filled with rows of cots, each one barely more than a metal frame with a thin, lumpy mattress. The air was musty, tinged with the smell of damp and unwashed linens. Mrs Hemmings pointed to a cot in the far corner.

"That's your bed," she said. "Make sure you keep it tidy. We run a tight ship here."

Mary walked slowly to the cot, her heart sinking further as she saw how uninviting it looked. The mattress was stained, and the blanket was thin and threadbare. She could already feel the dampness seeping through.

Mrs Hemmings stood in the doorway, her eyes cold. "You'll be sharing this room with twenty other girls. They're a tough lot, and you'll need to learn to fit in. Now, grow up and be a big girl. No more crying."

With that, she turned and left, the door closing behind her with a heavy thud. Mary sat on the edge of her cot, trying to hold back her tears. The room felt overwhelmingly large and yet claustrophobically crowded at the same time.

A few moments later, the other girls filed in after lunch. They ranged in age from young children to teenagers, and they all looked at Mary with a mix of curiosity and suspicion. Whispers filled the room as they settled onto their cots, but no one approached her.

Mary's tears began to fall again as she felt the weight of their stares and the loneliness of being in a strange new place. She hugged her knees to her chest, burying her face in her arms. The other girls, seeing her distress, turned away and resumed their activities, chatting amongst themselves and paying her no mind.

As the afternoon wore on, Mary remained on her cot, feeling more alone than ever. She missed her father, despite his flaws, and longed for the small comforts of their old life. The sounds of the girls talking and laughing around her only made her feel more isolated.

When evening came, the matron returned to oversee the bedtime routine. Mary lay down on the uncomfortable mattress, pulling the thin blanket over her. The room fell into an uneasy silence as the lights were extinguished, and Mary stared into the darkness, her heart heavy with grief and fear.

She knew she would have to be strong, just as Mrs Hemmings had said. For now, in the quiet of the night, she allowed herself to cry softly, hoping that somewhere, her father was thinking of her too.

***

The next morning, Mary was jolted awake by a gentle shake. Blinking sleepily, she looked up to see a girl about her age with kind eyes and a sympathetic smile.

"You'd better get up," the girl whispered. "If you're late for breakfast, Mrs Hemmings will have your hide."

Mary quickly scrambled out of bed, hurriedly straightening her rumpled clothes. "Thank you," she murmured, her voice still thick with sleep.

The girl nodded and led her to the dining hall, where rows of wooden tables were filled with children eating their breakfast. Mary joined the line and received a bowl of thin, watery porridge. She sat down and forced the tasteless meal down her throat, her stomach protesting at the blandness.

As she ate, she noticed a small group of girls being led away by a matron. Curious, she turned to the girl next to her. "Where are they going?" she asked.

The girl glanced at the departing group and then back at Mary. "Adoptive parents have come," she explained. "Some of the girls are lucky enough to be chosen."

Mary's eyes widened with a mix of hope and longing. "Do you think... do you think I might be chosen one day?"

The girl gave her a once-over, her expression turning sceptical. "I doubt it," she said bluntly. "You're too skinny and ugly. Families want healthy, pretty girls."

Mary's heart sank at the harsh words. She looked down at her thin arms and tattered dress, feeling a surge of despair. As the breakfast hall buzzed with chatter, Mary let her mind wander, imagining a different life.

In her daydream, she saw herself with a loving family. They lived in a warm, cosy house, with a garden where she could play. Her new parents were kind and gentle, and she had siblings who laughed and played with her. The house was filled with light and laughter, and Mary felt safe and cherished.

Another vision took hold, one where her father returned to take her home. He was no longer the broken, distant man she had known recently but the loving father she remembered from happier times. They lived together in a small but comfortable home, where they shared meals and stories, and Mary no longer felt lonely or afraid.

A sharp voice interrupted her reverie. "Stop daydreaming and finish your breakfast," one of the older girls snapped.

Mary quickly spooned the last of the porridge into her mouth, the reality of the orphanage crashing back down around her. As the meal ended and the children were herded off to their various chores, Mary felt a flicker of determination ignite within her.

No matter how hard things were, she would hold on to the hope that one day, she might find a family or be reunited with her father. That hope would keep her going through the difficult days ahead.

Chapter Three

One year passed before Mary was finally chosen to be considered by a possible family. In that time, she had hardly put on any weight, her frail frame a result of relentless chores she was always picked for. Scrubbing floors, washing laundry, and tending to the gruelling tasks that the other girls avoided left her perpetually tired and hungry.

One crisp morning, Mrs Hemmings called Mary to her office. Mary's heart leaped with a mixture of excitement and trepidation. As she stood before the matron, Mrs Hemmings regarded her with a critical eye.

"Mary," she said, "a family is coming to look at you today. They are good people, and if they choose you, you'll leave here and live with them."

Mary's initial excitement faded as the reality of the situation dawned on her. If she went with a new family, she would have to leave her father behind forever. Panic gripped her heart.

"My father," she said, her voice shaking. "He will come here for me. I know he will."

The other girls, who had gathered around to listen, began to murmur. One of them, a tall girl named Alice, hissed, "Quiet, Mary! Don't speak of such things."

Mary lifted her chin defiantly. "He will come. I'm sure of it."

Mrs Hemmings' eyes narrowed. "Enough of this nonsense," she snapped. "Your father left you here because he could not care for you. You will do well to remember that. Now, if you do not behave, I will have no choice but to take the belt to you."

Mary's eyes filled with tears, but she bit her lip and nodded. The other girls dispersed, casting her sympathetic but wary glances. She spent the rest of the morning scrubbing the dining hall floor, her mind a whirl of conflicting emotions. The hope of a new family battled with the loyalty she felt towards her father.

As lunchtime approached, the atmosphere in the orphanage grew tense. Word had spread that prospective parents were coming, and all the girls were on their best behaviour, their faces scrubbed clean and their clothes tidied.

Mary was called back to Mrs Hemmings' office just as the sun reached its highest point. She stood in the corner, her heart pounding in her chest. She could hear the muffled sounds of conversation from the other side of the door.

Finally, the door opened, and Mrs Hemmings ushered in a well-dressed couple. The woman wore a dark green dress with a delicate lace collar, and the man had a neatly trimmed moustache and a kind smile. They looked at Mary with warmth.

"This is Mary," Mrs Hemmings said, her voice unusually soft. "She is a good girl, though a bit thin."

The woman stepped forward, her eyes gentle. "Hello, Mary," she said. "We've heard a lot about you."

Mary looked up at the kind faces of the couple. Her heart ached with confusion and fear. "I don't want to go with you," she blurted out, her voice trembling. "My father... he'll come for me soon. I know he will."

The man exchanged a glance with his wife, his expression filled with understanding. "We know this is difficult," he said softly. "We want to give you a loving home, Mary."

Tears welled up in Mary's eyes. "No! You don't understand. I can't leave. I *won't* leave!" Her voice rose, filled with desperation.

Mrs Hemmings stepped forward, her face stern. "Mary, that's enough. These nice people are offering you a chance at a better life. You should be grateful."

Mary shook her head vehemently, backing away from the couple. "I don't want a new family! I want my father!"

The woman knelt down to Mary's level, trying to comfort her. "Sweetheart, sometimes parents can't take care of their children. It's not because they don't love them."

Mary's sobs grew louder, her small body shaking with the force of her emotions. "He will come back! He loves me!" She could barely get the words out between her cries.

The kind woman's face fell, and she glanced up at her husband, who looked equally troubled. "We understand, Mary," she said softly. "We'll give you time."

Mary was inconsolable. "I don't want time! I don't want you! I want my father!" She screamed, her voice echoing through the room.

Mrs Hemmings' patience wore thin. She grabbed Mary by the arm, pulling her away from the couple. "That is quite enough, young lady. You will not speak to adults in that manner."

Mary struggled against her grip, tears streaming down her face. "No! Let me go! Please, I don't want to go with them!"

Mrs Hemmings dragged her out of the study, her face a mask of cold anger. Once they were in the hallway, she leaned down, her voice low and threatening. "You will not be such a brat, Mary. You have no idea how fortunate you are that someone wants you. Now, you will go back to your chores and behave yourself."

Mary looked up at her, her eyes red and swollen from crying. "My father..."

"Your father isn't coming back," Mrs Hemmings said harshly. "You need to accept that and make the best of your situation."

Mary's heart shattered at the words. She felt utterly alone, abandoned by the one person she had always believed would return for her. As Mrs Hemmings marched her back to the dormitory, Mary's spirit felt as though it had been crushed beneath the weight of her despair.

After Mrs Hemmings left, the room fell into an uneasy silence. Mary lay on her cot, tears still wet on her cheeks, trying to stifle the sobs that threatened to escape. She felt a presence beside her and looked up to see Alice standing there, her arms crossed and her expression a mixture of sympathy and frustration.

"You've got to grow up, Mary," Alice said, her tone stern but not unkind. "If you want to fit in here, you need to stop acting like a baby."

Mary swallowed hard, trying to stop the fresh wave of tears. "I miss my daddy," she whispered, her voice breaking. "He said he'd come back for me."

Alice sighed and sat down on the edge of Mary's cot. "I know it's hard. We all miss our families. You have to understand, some of us have been here for years, hoping for a chance like the one you just threw away. So many girls are desperate for a family. How could you be so callous and ruin a perfectly good chance?"

Mary flinched at Alice's words, feeling a pang of guilt and shame. "I didn't mean to," she said softly. "I just... I thought he would come back."

Alice's face softened a bit. "I get it, I do. You've got to be realistic. We don't get many chances here. You can't just throw them away because of a dream that might never come true."

Mary nodded slowly, wiping her eyes with the back of her hand. "I'm sorry," she said, her voice barely above a whisper.

Alice stood up, her posture still firm. "Sorry doesn't fix things, Mary. You need to prove that you can be responsible. Now, get up and get on with your chores. Mrs Hemmings will be watching you closely after today."

Mary took a deep breath, forcing herself to stand. Her legs felt weak, and her heart was heavy, but she knew Alice was right. She couldn't afford to dwell on what she had lost. She had to focus on surviving in this place, on proving that she could be strong.

Alice gave her a small, encouraging nod. "That's it. One step at a time. Just get through today, and then the next day. It'll get easier."

Mary nodded again, feeling a flicker of determination amidst her sorrow. She walked over to the bucket and scrub brush by the door, picking them up with trembling hands. The other girls were already busy with their chores, and Mary knew she had to catch up.

As she scrubbed the floors, the repetitive motion helped to calm her racing thoughts. She focused on the task at hand, letting the work ground her. The pain of her father's absence was still there, but she pushed it aside, knowing she had to be strong.

The day wore on, and Mary found herself slowly settling into the routine. The other girls occasionally glanced her way, some with sympathy, others with indifference. She knew she had a long way to go to earn their trust and acceptance, but she was determined to try.

By the time the sun began to set, Mary was exhausted but felt a small sense of accomplishment. She had made it through the day without breaking down again. As she lay on her cot that night, she thought about her father, about the life she had lost, and the uncertain future ahead of her.

She whispered a silent promise to herself. "I'll be strong, Daddy. I'll make you proud."

With that thought, she drifted into a restless sleep, ready to face whatever challenges the next day would bring.

Chapter Four

One Year Later

A year had passed, and Mary, now twelve, had not been chosen to see a family again. She had grown accustomed to the routine of the orphanage, though the ache for her father never left her heart.

She did her chores diligently, her thin frame becoming stronger with each passing day, her spirit resilient despite the harshness of her environment. The other girls had come to accept her, and even Alice had become a sort of reluctant friend, though she never hesitated to remind Mary of the realities of their lives.

Then, just a few weeks before Christmas, a miracle seemed to happen. Mary was in the middle of scrubbing the dining hall floor when she heard her name called sharply. She looked up to see Mrs Hemmings standing in the doorway, her expression inscrutable.

"Mary, come with me," she said, and Mary followed, her heart pounding with a mixture of hope and fear.

They walked down the familiar corridor to the front office. As Mrs Hemmings opened the door, Mary saw a figure standing by the window, his back turned to her. Her breath caught in her throat. It couldn't be...

The man turned around, and Mary's heart leapt. Dark hair, broad nose. It was her father. He looked older, more worn than she remembered, but it was unmistakably him.

"Daddy?" she whispered, barely daring to believe it.

He nodded, a small, weary smile on his face. "Hello, Mary. I've come to take you home."

Mary felt a rush of joy and ran to him, throwing her arms around his waist. He hugged her back, though the embrace was brief and awkward. "I've missed you so much," she said, tears streaming down her face.

He patted her back awkwardly. "You're old enough to take care of yourself now," he stated. "You can help me around the house to earn your keep."

Mrs Hemmings cleared her throat, and they broke apart. "Mr Beckwith, you'll need to sign these papers," she said, handing him a stack of documents.

As he began to sign, Mrs Hemmings turned to Mary. "You'll need to gather your things. You're leaving today."

Mary nodded, her heart racing with excitement and nerves. She hurried to the dormitory and quickly packed her few belongings. The other girls watched her with a mixture of envy and sadness.

Alice approached her, crossing her arms. "So, your dad finally came back," she said, her tone neutral.

Mary nodded, trying to keep her emotions in check. "Yes, he did."

Alice's expression softened slightly. "Good luck, Mary."

"Oh," Mary said, giving Alice a quick hug. "He came back for me. I don't need luck."

She rushed back to the office, her small bag clutched tightly in her hand. Her father was waiting, the papers signed and handed back to Mrs Hemmings. He took her bag and led her out of the orphanage.

As they walked through the streets towards their new home, Mary noticed the changes in her father. His steps were slower, his shoulders hunched with the weight of life's burdens. She was too happy to question it.

When they reached the small, cramped apartment, Mary's excitement dimmed slightly. It was far from the cosy home she had imagined. The place was dingy and cluttered, with a stale smell lingering in the air. It was now her home, and she was with her father again.

Over the next few days, it became clear why her father had taken her back. She was old enough now to cook meals, clean the house, and do the laundry.

It wasn't what she wanted. But being a family again, even in this way, was better than being unwanted and abandoned.

Mary's initial excitement at being reunited with her father quickly waned as the days passed. Her father's demeanour grew increasingly cold and detached, and it became clear that his main reason for taking her back was to have someone to manage the household chores.

Every morning, Mary woke up early to prepare breakfast, a simple meal of porridge or stale bread. Her father rarely spoke to her, his gruff instructions and occasional grunts of approval the only interaction they shared. She scrubbed the floors, washed the laundry, and cleaned the small, dingy home.

The weight of her responsibilities settled heavily on her small shoulders, but she bore it without complaint, determined to prove herself useful.

As Christmas approached, Mary tried to inject some cheer into their lives. She found some scraps of fabric and old bits of ribbon and made makeshift ornaments. She hung them around the apartment, hoping to bring some festive spirit to their lives. Her father barely noticed; his focus on his own troubles and the bottle that often accompanied him in the evenings.

One evening, as Mary was cleaning the kitchen, she gathered her courage and approached her father, who was sitting at the small table, staring into his mug.

"Daddy," she began hesitantly, "Christmas is coming. Do you think we could maybe do something special? Even if it's just a little?"

Her father looked up, his eyes bloodshot and tired. He let out a bitter laugh. "Special? Mary, we don't have money for special. We're barely getting by as it is."

Mary's heart sank, but she forced a smile. "I know, Daddy. I just thought maybe we could make the day nice somehow. Maybe have a nice meal together…"

He shook his head, his expression hardening. "We can't afford a roast goose or any of that nonsense. You should be grateful you have a roof over your head."

Mary nodded, swallowing the lump in her throat. "I am grateful, Daddy. I just thought…" Her voice trailed off as she realised any further protest would be futile.

As Christmas Eve day arrived, it passed by like any other day. There were no presents, and no festive cheer. Mary prepared a simple breakfast and watched as her father ate in silence, his face devoid of any emotion. She tried to keep her spirits up, reminding herself that at least they were together, even if the circumstances were far from what she had hoped for.

After breakfast, Mary went about her usual chores. She scrubbed the floors, washed the dishes, and did the laundry. She hummed Christmas carols softly to herself, trying to keep a positive attitude. Despite the coldness of their home, she clung to the hope that things might improve.

When Christmas Day arrived, it felt like any other day. Mary woke up to find her father already gone, having left for the docks before she was awake. Her heart sank with disappointment, but she pushed the feeling aside and set about her tasks. She scrubbed the kitchen floor, washed the meagre pile of dishes, and hung the laundry to dry. The routine was familiar, a small comfort in the otherwise bleak day.

By the afternoon, Mary had finished her chores. She sat by the fire, which was barely more than a few glowing embers, and watched the snow fall outside the window. The apartment was cold, the drafts seeping through the thin walls and making her shiver. She wrapped her mother's old shawl around her shoulders and hugged her knees to her chest.

Tears welled up in her eyes as she stared at the falling snow. She had hoped that, despite their lack of money, they could at least spend the day together. She had imagined sitting by the fire with her father, perhaps sharing a simple meal and talking.

He had left without a word, treating the day like any other. The realisation that her father didn't care about her, that he just wanted someone around to do the chores, cut deeply into her heart.

The hours dragged on, and the small apartment grew darker as evening fell. Mary lit a candle and set it on the table, its flickering light casting shadows on the walls. She prepared a simple dinner, keeping it warm as long as she could, hoping her father would come home soon. When he finally arrived, it was long after dark, and the food had gone cold.

Mary stood up as he walked in, the smell of ale and tobacco wafting into the room. "Daddy, where have you been?" she asked, trying to keep the worry out of her voice. "I made dinner."

He looked at her with bloodshot eyes, his expression sour. "That's none of your business," he snapped. "You're a child. Don't ask questions."

Mary flinched at his harsh tone. "I was just worried," she said quietly. "I thought we could spend Christmas together."

Her father scowled, his breath reeking of alcohol. "Christmas? I've been working, trying to keep a roof over our heads. Be grateful for that."

Tears pricked at Mary's eyes, but she blinked them away. "I am grateful, Daddy. I just... I thought we could have a little bit of time together."

He waved her off dismissively and sat down at the table, shoving the cold food into his mouth without a word of thanks. Mary watched him, her heart aching with a mix of love and disappointment. She realised then that her father had changed irrevocably, and the man who once cared for her was gone. He saw her now only as a convenience, someone to cook his meals and keep his house clean.

When he finished eating, he stood up and stumbled towards his bedroom, leaving the empty plate on the table. Mary sighed and cleared it away, washing it along with the rest of the dishes. She moved mechanically, her mind numb.

After tidying up, she returned to her spot by the fire, watching the last of the embers glow faintly. The snow continued to fall outside, and Mary wrapped the shawl tighter around her, seeking solace in its familiar warmth. She knew that things were unlikely to change, but she resolved to find strength within herself.

She whispered a quiet prayer, her breath visible in the cold air. "Please, let things get better. Help me to be strong."

With that, she blew out the candle and retreated to her small bed, pulling the thin blanket over herself. The apartment was silent, save for the distant sounds of the city. Mary closed her eyes, her thoughts a mix of memories of happier times and the harsh reality of her present life.

As she drifted off to sleep, she clung to the hope that somehow, someday, things would improve. She dreamed of a future where she was no longer a burden or her father's maid, but someone cherished and loved. Until then, she would endure, finding strength in the small moments of peace and the faint glimmers of hope that kept her spirit alive.

Chapter Five

The next morning, Mary woke to find the apartment cold and silent. Her father had already left for the docks, as he always did, without a word. She sighed and pushed herself out of bed, the chill biting at her skin. She dressed quickly in her worn clothes and headed to the kitchen.

Mary decided to start with the laundry. She hated doing it, so she liked to get it out of the way first. Gathering the dirty clothes, she hauled them to the washbasin and began scrubbing. The water was icy, and her hands quickly turned numb, but she worked diligently, her mind wandering to distract herself from the discomfort.

As she wrung out the clothes and hung them to dry, she heard the distant sound of children laughing and playing in the snow outside. She paused for a moment, listening to their joyful voices, a pang of longing piercing her heart. She missed the carefree days when she could play outside without a worry, but those days felt like a distant memory now.

Mary forced herself to focus on her work. She had no time for such indulgences. Besides, the only friend she had ever made at the orphanage was Alice, and she had likely been adopted by now, living a better life far from here. Mary shook off the melancholy thoughts and returned to her chores.

With the laundry done, she set about making breakfast. She prepared the same simple porridge, stirring it slowly as it cooked. The apartment remained cold and uninviting, the thin walls doing little to keep out the winter chill. She poured the porridge into a bowl and sat down at the small table, eating in silence.

After breakfast, Mary cleaned up and began tidying the rest of the home. She swept the floors, dusted the sparse furniture, and made sure everything was in order. Her routine was a familiar comfort, a way to keep her mind occupied and stave off the loneliness that threatened to overwhelm her.

As she worked, her thoughts drifted back to the sounds of the children outside. She couldn't help but imagine what it would be like to join them, to feel the snow under her feet and the cold air on her face. But she knew better than to entertain such fantasies.

Her life was here, in this small house, taking care of her father and managing the household chores.

By midday, the apartment was clean, and Mary allowed herself a brief moment of rest. She sat by the window, watching the snow continue to fall. The world outside seemed so different from her own, filled with laughter and joy that felt out of reach. She wrapped her mother's shawl around her shoulders, finding comfort in its familiar warmth.

The day passed slowly, each hour marked by the steady rhythm of her chores. As evening approached, Mary prepared dinner, keeping it simple but as hearty as their meagre supplies allowed. She set the table and waited, hoping her father would come home soon.

When he finally returned, it was late, and he looked as weary as ever. He said nothing as he sat down at the table, and Mary served him his dinner. The food was cold by now, and she saw the displeasure in his eyes as he took a bite.

"Where have you been this time, Daddy?" she asked cautiously, trying to keep her voice steady.

He glanced at her, his expression darkening. "Working, Mary. Like I always do," he muttered, his voice rough.

Mary bit her lip, unsure whether to press further. "It's so late."

"Yes. And?"

"Daddy," Mary began, her voice trembling, "I just want to understand. Why do you always come home so late? Why do you smell like... like ale?"

His face flushed with anger. "You don't need to understand anything, Mary. You're a child. You do as you're told and keep your mouth shut."

Mary felt a surge of frustration and sadness. "I just miss you, Daddy. I miss how things used to be."

Her father slammed his fist on the table, making the dishes rattle. "I said enough!" he roared. "Go to your room. Now."

Mary recoiled, her eyes wide with fear. She had never seen him this angry or drunk before. Tears welled up in her eyes as she stood up, her legs trembling. "I'm sorry, Daddy," she whispered, her voice barely audible.

He didn't respond, his gaze fixed on the table. Mary turned and fled to her small room, closing the door behind her. She leaned against it, her heart pounding in her chest. The tears she had been holding back finally spilled over, and she sank to the floor, sobbing quietly.

As she sat there, her mind raced with thoughts and emotions. She had spent so much time wishing for her father to come back, to take her away from the orphanage. Now, faced with his anger and drunkenness, she felt more alone than ever.

For the first time, she allowed herself to think that perhaps she had been better off at the orphanage. Despite the harshness of Mrs Hemmings and the endless chores, there had been a sense of structure and predictability. Alice had been a friend, a source of comfort in the bleakness.

Mary hugged her knees to her chest, rocking back and forth as she cried. The hope and excitement she had felt at being reunited with her father were now replaced with a deep sense of despair. She longed for the warmth and love she had lost, but it seemed further away than ever.

Eventually, her sobs quieted, and she wiped her eyes with the back of her hand. She knew she had to be strong, to endure whatever came her way. But the weight of her father's anger and the coldness of their home felt almost too much to bear.

Mary crawled into bed, pulling the thin blanket over herself. She whispered a silent prayer, asking for strength and guidance. As she drifted off to sleep, her thoughts were filled with memories of happier times and the faint hope that one day, things might get better.

The following morning, she woke up to find the house empty once again. Her father had already left for the docks, leaving her to face another day of chores and solitude. Mary sighed and got out of bed, determined to get through the day as best she could. The dream of a better life remained a distant glimmer, but it was enough to keep her going, even in the darkest of times.

Chapter Six

The next week, Mary's father missed a day of work because he was hung over. Mary found him sprawled on his bed, the room filled with the sour stench of alcohol. She tried to rouse him gently, her small hands shaking him.

"Daddy, you need to go to work," she whispered urgently, but he only groaned and turned away.

As she left him to sleep off his stupor, Mary's worry grew. She knew how important his job at the docks was. If he lost it, they would have nothing. The thought gnawed at her throughout the day as she went about her chores, the fear of their precarious situation ever-present in her mind.

Fortunately, her father did not lose his job that day, which was a small consolation to Mary. His frequent absences and diminished wages meant that Mary had to stretch their food budget as far as it could go. She became adept at making simple meals with the scant supplies they had, often going without herself to ensure her father had enough to eat.

One afternoon, as Mary scrubbed the floor, she thought about the last few weeks. The joy she had felt when her father had taken her from the orphanage had quickly been overshadowed by the harsh reality of their life together. Her father's drinking and his neglect weighed heavily on her young shoulders.

That evening, Mary prepared a thin soup with the last of the vegetables she had managed to buy. She served it in their chipped bowls, hoping it would be enough to sustain them. Her father sat at the table, his face pale and drawn. He ate in silence, and Mary watched him, her heart aching.

"Daddy," she said quietly, "you need to be careful. If you miss too many days at work, you might lose your job."

He looked up at her, his eyes bloodshot and tired. "I know, Mary," he muttered. "I'm doing my best."

She wanted to believe him, but the evidence of his actions told a different story. She nodded, not wanting to upset him further. "I'll make sure we have enough food," she said, trying to sound confident.

As they sat in silence, Mary couldn't help but feel a surge of frustration. She took a deep breath, trying to keep her voice steady. "Daddy, why did you even bother getting me back from the orphanage if things were going to be like this?"

Her father's eyes darkened, and he set his fork down with a sharp clatter. "What did you just say?"

Mary's heart pounded in her chest, but she pressed on. "You barely talk to me. You're always angry. I try to help, but it feels like it's never enough. Why did you bring me back?"

He stood up abruptly, his chair scraping against the floor. "You're being ungrateful, Mary. I brought you back because you're my daughter. You should be thankful for that."

"I am grateful," she said, her voice rising. "It's just so hard. You don't see what it's like for me. You don't listen."

"Don't listen?" he shouted. "I listen to you whining every day. You think it's easy for me? Your mother didn't raise you to be selfish."

The mention of her mother made Mary's eyes fill with tears. "Mama isn't here, Daddy. She wouldn't want to see us like this. She wouldn't want us to be so angry and sad."

He stared at her, his expression a mix of anger and pain. "Just leave me alone, Mary."

Mary felt a lump in her throat. "Fine," she said quietly, her voice barely above a whisper. She turned and walked to the door, pulling on her worn coat. She stepped outside, the cold air biting at her skin.

She stood in the little courtyard, feeling the snowflakes land softly on her face. The chill seeped through her clothes, but she didn't care. The fresh air was a welcome relief from the stifling atmosphere inside. She looked up at the darkening sky, wondering how Alice was doing. Had she been adopted? Was she happy?

Mary thought about Mrs Hemmings and the orphanage. Despite the strict rules and the hard work, there had been a sense of stability there, a structure to her days that was now missing. Did they miss her? Did they wonder what had become of her?

She sat down on a cold stone bench, pulling her coat tighter around her. The courtyard was silent; the only sound the soft whisper of falling snow. Mary's thoughts drifted to happier times, to memories of her mother's gentle touch and her father's warm laughter. Those days felt so far away now, almost like a dream.

As she sat there, alone in the cold, Mary allowed herself to cry. The tears came slowly at first, then faster, until she was sobbing into her hands. She cried for her lost family, for the harsh reality of her life, and for the uncertainty of her future.

After a while, she wiped her eyes and took a deep breath, trying to steady herself. She knew she couldn't stay out there forever. She had to go back inside, face her father, and continue doing her best. For now, she allowed herself this moment of solitude, a brief escape.

Eventually, the cold drove Mary back inside. She opened the door quietly and slipped into the dimly lit apartment. Her father was sitting at the dining table with a bottle of something strong, the fumes of alcohol filling the room.

He looked up when she entered, his eyes narrowing. "Where've you been?" he slurred, his voice thick with anger. "Think you can just walk out whenever you want?"

Mary kept her head down, moving straight to the kitchen to start on the dishes. "I just needed some fresh air," she said softly, not wanting to provoke him further.

He took a swig from the bottle, watching her with a suspicious glare. "You think you can ignore me, eh? Think you're too good to talk to your old man?"

Mary didn't respond, focusing on the task at hand. She knew from experience that arguing back would only make things worse. The clatter of dishes and water provided a steady, soothing rhythm that helped her block out his words.

"Answer me, girl!" he shouted, slamming his fist on the table. "Don't you dare ignore me!"

Mary's hands trembled as she scrubbed a pot, but she kept her voice steady. "I'm not ignoring you, Daddy. I'm just doing the dishes."

His eyes blazed with anger. "You think you're so smart, don't you? Think you know better than me?"

She remained silent, her heart pounding in her chest. It took all her willpower to keep from responding, to stay calm and focused on the dishes. She knew this was the only way to avoid escalating the situation.

Her father stood up unsteadily, knocking over his chair. "You're just like your mother," he spat, his voice venomous. "Always thinking you're better than everyone else."

Mary bit her lip, forcing herself to remain calm. The words stung, but she knew they were from his frustration and pain. She took a deep breath and continued washing the dishes, her movements steady and deliberate.

After a few minutes of ranting, her father seemed to tire of the one-sided argument. He swayed on his feet, his anger dissipating into weariness. "Fine," he muttered. "Be that way. I'm going to bed."

He stumbled towards his bedroom, leaving the bottle on the table. Mary listened to the sound of his footsteps, the creak of the door, and the thud as he collapsed onto his bed. The room grew quiet once more, save for the faint sound of his snores.

Mary finished the dishes, her hands aching from the cold water and scrubbing. She dried them carefully and put them away, then tidied the kitchen and dining area. The empty bottle glinted in the dim light.

Once everything was in order, Mary allowed herself a moment to sit at the table.

She stared at the flickering candle, feeling the weight of the day's events pressing down on her. The reality of her situation was harsh and unforgiving, but she knew she had to endure.

She thought about the courtyard and the brief respite it had offered. She wondered if Alice was somewhere warm and safe, with a family who cared for her. She thought about Mrs Hemmings and the orphanage, where despite the strict rules, there had been a sense of community and structure.

Mary sighed and stood up, blowing out the candle. She moved quietly through the apartment, checking on her father one last time before heading to her own small room. The air was cold, and she wrapped herself tightly in her thin blanket, seeking warmth and comfort.

As she lay there, staring at the ceiling, she whispered a silent prayer. "Please, let things get better. Help me to be strong."

Chapter Seven

The summer heat was relentless, pressing down on the city with an unforgiving intensity. The small apartment became a stifling oven, the air thick and suffocating. Mary did her best to keep cool, but her worries were ever-present. Her father's drinking had only increased, and she feared that the heat combined with his alcohol consumption would make him ill.

One particularly sweltering afternoon, Mary found her father sprawled on the floor, an empty bottle by his side. Panic surged through her as she rushed to his side, shaking him gently. "Daddy, wake up. Please, wake up."

He groaned, his eyes fluttering open. "What do you want, Mary?" he muttered, his voice slurred.

"You need to drink water," she said, her voice trembling. "It's too hot, and you'll get sick."

He pushed her away weakly. "I'm fine. Leave me be."

Mary fetched a cup of water and held it to his lips. "Please, just drink. For me."

He reluctantly took a few sips, and Mary sighed with relief. She stayed by his side, wiping the sweat from his forehead and praying that the heat would break soon.

***

As the oppressive heat of summer faded into a distant memory, the biting cold of winter took its place. The apartment was icy cold, and they didn't have enough firewood to keep the fire going. Mary wrapped herself in layers of clothing, but the chill seeped through, making her shiver uncontrollably.

One evening, as the wind howled outside, Mary huddled by the small fireplace, trying to coax a few remaining embers back to life. Her father sat nearby, a bottle in his hand, his face shadowed and withdrawn.

"We need more firewood," Mary said quietly. "We'll freeze if we don't get any."

He looked at her, his eyes dull. "There's no money for firewood."

Mary's heart sank. "Maybe I can find some scraps in the alley," she suggested.

He nodded absently, and Mary bundled up before venturing outside. The cold bit at her skin, and her breath came out in visible puffs. She searched the alleyways, gathering whatever bits of wood and debris she could find.

When she returned, she managed to get a small fire going, enough to take the edge off the cold. As she warmed her hands by the flickering flames, she glanced at her father, hoping for a sign of gratitude or acknowledgement. He remained silent, lost in his own world.

***

The bitter cold of winter reminded Mary of the sense of community and structure she had once known at the orphanage. One particularly harsh day, she found herself standing in front of the familiar building, her heart pounding with a mix of fear and longing. She hadn't seen Alice or Mrs Hemmings in years, and the thought of going inside filled her with both hope and dread.

She took a step forward, then hesitated. What if they didn't remember her? What if they were angry that she had left? The questions swirled in her mind, paralysing her with indecision.

Mary stood there for what felt like an eternity, her eyes fixed on the orphanage's doors. She longed to see Alice, to find out if her friend had found a better life. But the fear of rejection kept her rooted to the spot.

Finally, she turned away, her heart heavy with regret. She walked back to the apartment, the shadows of her past following her every step.

***

As the days grew colder, the tension between Mary and her father escalated. One bitterly cold morning, Mary was jolted awake by the sound of the door creaking open. She glanced at the clock: six in the morning. Her father stumbled in, reeking of alcohol, his clothes dishevelled and his eyes bloodshot.

"Daddy, where have you been?" she asked, her voice a mix of worry and frustration.

He waved her off, staggering towards the kitchen. "None of your business, Mary."

Tears welled up in her eyes as she followed him. "It is my business! You were gone all night. I was worried sick!"

He spun around, his face contorted with anger. "I don't need to explain myself to you! You're just a child."

"I'm not a child anymore," she shot back, her voice trembling with emotion. "I'm the one who takes care of everything while you're out drinking."

He raised his hand as if to strike her, then let it fall to his side. "You don't understand anything."

Mary stepped back, her heart pounding. "Mama wouldn't want this. She wouldn't want us to be like this."

He stared at her, his anger fading into a look of deep sadness. "Leave me alone, Mary," he said, his voice breaking.

She watched him slump into a chair, defeated and broken. Without another word, she turned and walked outside, the cold morning air biting at her skin. She sat in the small courtyard, hugging her knees to her chest, tears streaming down her face.

As she gazed up at the slowly brightening sky, she wondered if Alice ever thought about her, if Mrs Hemmings remembered the quiet girl who had once hoped for a better life.

Finally, she stood up, brushed the snow from her clothes, and went back inside. Her father had passed out at the table, the bottle still clutched in his hand. Mary sighed and took the bottle away, then covered him with a blanket. She finished her morning chores in silence, the house growing colder with each passing hour. Despite everything, she held onto the hope that one day, things might change for the better.

***

Mary's fourteenth birthday passed without mention, just like any other day. She spent most of it in her small room, the silence weighing heavily on her. The walls seemed to close in, a stark reminder of her isolation. She knew better than to expect any acknowledgment from her father; he hadn't remembered her birthday in years.

She sat on her bed, staring out the window at the grey sky, lost in her thoughts. She tried to focus on the memories of happier birthdays when her mother was still alive, but they felt like distant dreams. Her father's heavy footsteps echoed through the apartment, a constant reminder of the volatile presence that kept her in check.

Mary didn't dare leave her room, fearing that any interaction might lead to anger or disappointment. She heard the clink of bottles from the other room, and her heart sank further. As the day faded into night, she lay on her bed, tears silently rolling down her cheeks, whispering a birthday wish into the darkness.

A few weeks later, on a rare trip to the market, Mary saw a little girl playing hopscotch on the street. The girl's laughter was infectious, her small feet skipping from square to square with carefree joy. Mary paused, watching her, a pang of longing gripping her heart.

She wished she could be that little girl, unburdened by the weight of adult responsibilities. The simple game seemed like a world away from her reality. She remembered playing hopscotch with Alice in the courtyard of the orphanage, their laughter echoing off the walls.

Mary sighed and turned away, carrying her meagre purchases back to the apartment. The sight of the little girl's happiness stayed with her, a bittersweet reminder of what she had lost and what she still yearned for.

**

One chilly afternoon, as Mary was walking back from the market, she saw a girl with blonde hair ahead of her. Her heart skipped a beat. Could it be Alice? She quickened her pace, hope blossoming in her chest.

"Excuse me!" Mary called out, her voice trembling with anticipation. The girl turned around, and Mary's heart sank. It wasn't Alice. The girl gave her a puzzled look before walking away, leaving Mary standing in the middle of the street, feeling foolish and disappointed.

She watched the girl disappear into the crowd, her hope fading as quickly as it had come. Mary wrapped her shawl tighter around her shoulders and continued her journey home, the familiar ache of loneliness settling in once more.

**

Mary's fifteenth birthday dawned with a glimmer of hope. Her father had gone to work sober, and for the first time in a long while, she dared to believe that things might be looking up. She cleaned the apartment meticulously, preparing a simple meal for dinner, hoping they could share a quiet, peaceful evening together.

As the day wore on, she glanced at the clock anxiously, waiting for her father to return. The hours passed slowly, and the shadows lengthened in the small apartment. Dinner grew cold on the table, and Mary's hope began to wane.

When night fell and he still hadn't returned, Mary's heart filled with a familiar sense of dread. She sat by the window, watching the darkness deepen outside, her fingers tracing patterns on the frosted glass. Her stomach knotted with worry and disappointment.

Finally, she couldn't wait any longer. She cleared the untouched dinner from the table and washed the dishes in silence. She prepared for bed, the apartment eerily quiet. As she lay down, she whispered a birthday wish, hoping against hope that things would change.

Mary woke several times during the night, listening for the sound of the door, but it never came. She finally drifted into a fitful sleep, the weight of her fifteenth birthday pressing heavily on her heart. She faced another year of struggle and loneliness, but she resolved to hold onto the faint glimmers of hope that kept her spirit alive. Despite the hardships, she knew she had to keep going, for there was always the possibility that one day, things might truly get better.

Chapter Eight

A week after her fifteenth birthday, Mary was scrubbing the floor when there was a sudden, sharp knock on the door. She froze, her heart leaping into her throat. Her mind raced with possibilities, most of them bad. Was it her father, drunk and unable to find his keys? Or had something worse happened?

She wiped her hands on her apron and cautiously opened the door. Two police officers stood there, their expressions sombre. Mary's heart sank, and she gripped the doorframe for support.

"Are you Mary Beckwith?" one of the officers asked gently.

"Yes," she replied, her voice barely above a whisper. "Is something wrong? Has my father...?"

The officer nodded gravely. "May we come in?"

Mary stepped aside, her mind reeling. They entered the small apartment, their presence making the space feel even smaller and more oppressive. She gestured for them to sit, but they remained standing.

"What happened?" Mary asked, her voice trembling.

The officer who had spoken before sighed. "I'm very sorry to have to tell you this, but your father has been in an accident at the docks."

Mary's heart pounded in her chest. "An accident! Is he... is he hurt?"

The second officer, a man with kind eyes, stepped forward. "I'm afraid he didn't survive, Mary. He passed away at the scene."

The words hit Mary like a physical blow, and she staggered back, nearly falling. She couldn't breathe. The room spun around her, and she felt a wave of dizziness.

"No," she whispered, tears streaming down her face. "No, this can't be happening."

The officer reached out a hand to steady her. "I'm so sorry for your loss. We know this is a terrible shock."

Mary sank to her knees, sobbing uncontrollably. Her father was gone. Despite all the hardships, despite the drinking and the arguments, he had been her only family. The only connection she had to her family, to her mother. Now he was gone.

The officers waited patiently, giving her time to process the news. Mary felt like her world was collapsing around her. She clutched at the hem of her apron, her knuckles white.

"How did it happen?" she managed to ask between sobs.

The officer cleared his throat. "There was an accident with some of the machinery at the docks. It's a dangerous place, and sometimes... sometimes these things happen. It was quick, Mary. He didn't suffer."

Mary nodded numbly, the details blurring in her mind. Her father was dead. She was alone.

"Is there anyone we can fetch for you?" the officer asked gently. "Any family or friends?"

Mary shook her head. "No. There's no one."

The officers exchanged a look of concern. "There are services that can help you during this difficult time."

Mary took the card with shaking hands, barely seeing it through her tears. "Thank you," she whispered, though the words felt hollow.

The officers stayed a moment longer, offering their condolences again before finally taking their leave. Mary closed the door behind them and leaned against it, sliding down to the floor. She hugged her knees to her chest, rocking back and forth as sobs wracked her body.

Her father was gone. The man who had been a source of both pain and comfort, her only remaining family, was dead. She felt an overwhelming sense of loss, a void that seemed impossible to fill.

As the shock slowly began to subside, another thought crept into her mind, bringing with it a new wave of panic. What would she do now? She had no money, no support, and no way to pay for the rent or food. She was only fifteen, but she knew she needed to find a job, and quickly.

Wiping her tears, Mary forced herself to stand. Her legs felt weak, but she steeled herself. She couldn't afford to fall apart. Not now. She needed to survive, just as she always had. She had to be strong, for herself and for the memory of her parents.

She took a deep breath, trying to calm the storm of emotions inside her. The task ahead seemed insurmountable, but she had no choice. She would find a job; she would find a way to keep going. Because she had to. There was no other option.

***

The next morning, Mary lay in bed, the weight of grief pressing heavily on her chest. She pulled the thin blanket over her head, wishing she could hide from the world. The reality of her father's death was a crushing blow, and the thought of facing the day felt impossible. Tears streamed down her face as she buried her sobs in the pillow.

Then she remembered the old matron, her stern voice echoing in her mind. "Stop crying and be a big girl, Mary." She had heard those words countless times, and now they resonated with a new urgency. Mary wiped her tears, took a deep breath, and forced herself to sit up. She couldn't afford to stay in bed. She had to be strong.

She dressed quickly, her hands trembling as she buttoned her worn dress. She glanced around the small apartment, its emptiness more pronounced than ever. She grabbed a piece of bread from the kitchen, barely tasting it as she ate, her mind focused on the daunting task ahead.

Mary stepped out into the cold morning air, her breath visible in the chill. She walked through the streets, stopping at several shops and grocers, each time mustering the courage to ask for work. Each time, she was met with the same response—shaking heads and polite refusals.

At an inn, she approached the innkeeper with a hopeful heart. "Excuse me, sir. Are you looking for any help? I'm willing to do any work you have."

The innkeeper, a burly man with a kind face, sighed sympathetically. "Sorry, lass. We're fully staffed at the moment. Try again next month, maybe."

Mary nodded, her hope dwindling with each rejection. She walked aimlessly, her feet carrying her through the bustling streets. She felt lost and overwhelmed, on the brink of despair.

As she stood on a corner, wondering where to go next, a kindly woman approached her. She had noticed Mary's desperate search and offered a warm smile. "You look like you're in need of work, dear."

Mary nodded, her voice barely above a whisper. "Yes, ma'am. I've been looking all morning."

The woman placed a gentle hand on Mary's shoulder. "I heard that Mr Everly is looking for scullery staff. His townhouse is just down the road, the one with the green shutters. Give it a try."

Mary's heart leaped with a renewed sense of hope. "Thank you so much," she said, her voice trembling with gratitude.

The woman nodded kindly and walked away, leaving Mary with a sense of direction. She hurried down the road, her eyes scanning the buildings until she spotted the townhouse with the green shutters. It was a grand house, well-kept and imposing, but Mary pushed her nerves aside and approached the door.

She knocked hesitantly, her hands shaking. After a moment, the door opened, revealing a middle-aged woman with a stern, but not unkind, face.

"Can I help you?" the woman asked, her eyes appraising Mary.

Mary took a deep breath. "I heard that Mr Everly is looking for scullery staff. I'm very willing to work hard, ma'am."

The woman looked Mary over, her expression thoughtful. "Wait here," she said, then disappeared inside.

Mary stood on the doorstep, her heart pounding in her chest. She clutched her hands together, praying silently for a chance. After what felt like an eternity, the woman returned, a slight smile on her face.

"Come in," she said. "Mr Everly will see you now."

Mary followed her inside, the warmth of the house a stark contrast to the cold outside. She was led through a hallway and into a spacious, well-furnished room where Mr Everly sat behind a large desk.

The man looked up as Mary entered, his eyes sharp but not unkind. He had dusty brown hair and sharp features, but there was a softness in his gaze. "So, you're looking for work?"

"Yes, sir," Mary replied, her voice steady. "I'm willing to do any task you need."

Mr Everly leaned back in his chair, studying her for a moment. "What's your name, and how old are you?"

"Mary Beckwith, sir. I'm fifteen."

He nodded, tapping his fingers on the desk. "Have you worked in a household before?"

"Yes, sir. I've taken care of my father's home for several years. I can clean, cook, and manage household chores."

Mr Everly exchanged a glance with the woman who had answered the door. She nodded subtly, and he turned back to Mary. "Very well. You can start tomorrow. Mrs Cartwright here will show you your duties."

Mary's heart soared with relief and gratitude. "Thank you, sir. I won't let you down."

Mr Everly nodded. "I trust you won't. Be here at dawn, and be ready to work hard."

Mary nodded, her voice filled with determination. "Yes, sir. Thank you again."

As she left the townhouse, Mary's heart flooded with relief. She had found a job, a way to support herself, but the reality of her father's death and the new responsibilities ahead weighed heavily on her. Still, she resolved to face whatever came her way with the strength and resilience that had carried her through so much already. She packed what little belongings she had, knowing that she'd have to leave the apartment. But she looked forward to her new job and life at the Everly household.

Chapter Nine

The next day, Mary arrived at Mr Everly's townhouse at the crack of dawn, her heart pounding with determination. She knocked on the door, and Mrs Cartwright opened it with a warm smile.

"Good morning, Mary. Come in," she said, stepping aside to let Mary enter. "We have much to do today."

Mary followed Mrs Cartwright down the hall and into the kitchen, where several maids were bustling about. The kitchen was large and well-equipped, with the scent of freshly baked bread filling the air. Mrs Cartwright gathered the maids and introduced Mary.

"Girls, this is Mary Beckwith. She'll be joining us as a scullery maid," Mrs Cartwright announced.

The maids, mostly girls a bit older than Mary, turned to look at her. They were clearly friends, exchanging knowing glances and polite smiles. Mary felt a pang of self-consciousness, but she straightened her shoulders and forced a smile.

One of the maids, a tall girl with dark hair named Lizzie, gave Mary a once-over. "Welcome, Mary. We'll show you what to do," she said, her tone friendly enough but with an underlying hint of amusement.

"Thank you," Mary replied, her voice steady.

Mrs Cartwright handed Mary an apron and led her to the sink filled with dirty dishes. "You'll start here, Mary. Wash these and make sure they're spotless. We have high standards in this house."

Mary nodded eagerly. "Yes, ma'am. I'll do my best."

She rolled up her sleeves and plunged her hands into the soapy water, scrubbing the dishes with fervour. As she worked, she listened to the chatter of the other maids, feeling a bit like an outsider. They seemed to know each other well, talking in hushed whispers.

One of the maids, a cheerful girl with bright red hair, approached Mary with a smile. "I'm Annie. Need any help?"

Mary shook her head. "No, thank you. I've got it."

Annie nodded. "All right, just let us know if you do. We were all new once."

Mary smiled gratefully and continued working. She scrubbed pots and pans, washed plates and cutlery, and wiped down the counters, determined to prove herself. Her hands grew red and raw from the hot water, but she didn't slow down. She moved with purpose, her focus unwavering.

Mrs Cartwright watched her with an approving eye. "You're doing well, Mary," she said. "But you will need to do better to earn your place here."

"I will, Mrs Cartwright," Mary replied, her heart lifting at the praise.

The morning passed in a blur of activity. Mary scrubbed floors, polished silverware, and helped prepare vegetables for the evening meal. She worked tirelessly, her mind focused on each task. She wanted to show that she was capable, that she belonged there.

When lunchtime arrived, Mary was exhausted but satisfied with her efforts. She took a brief break to eat a piece of bread and some cheese, then resumed her work with renewed vigour.

As the day drew to a close, the kitchen buzzed with activity as the maids prepared the dinner for the Everly family. Mary helped where she could, her hands moving quickly and efficiently. She was determined to prove herself, to earn her place in this household.

When dinner was finally served, Mrs Cartwright gathered the staff. "All right, everyone. You've worked hard today. There are plenty of leftovers, so help yourselves."

Mary's stomach growled with anticipation as she filled her plate with roast beef, potatoes, and fresh vegetables. The aroma was heavenly, and her mouth watered as she took her first bite. The food was delicious, better than anything she had eaten in a long time.

For the first time in what felt like forever, Mary ate a full meal. She savoured every bite, feeling a warmth spread through her that had nothing to do with the food. She had worked hard, and she was being rewarded. It was a simple but profound feeling of accomplishment.

As she finished her meal, Mary looked around at the other maids, who were chatting and laughing. She still felt like an outsider, but the kindness of Mrs Cartwright and the hearty meal had given her a sense of belonging she hadn't felt in a long time.

That night, as Mary lay in the small bed provided for the maids, she thought about the day. It had been hard work, but she was proud of what she had achieved. She knew she had a long way to go to truly fit in, but she was determined to keep proving herself. She whispered a silent thank you to the stars visible through the tiny window, feeling a glimmer of hope for the future.

Chapter Ten

At seventeen, Mary stood in the grand hallway of Mr Everly's townhouse, her heart pounding with excitement. Mrs Cartwright had called her to the parlour, and Mary could hardly contain her nerves. Over the years, she had worked diligently, climbing her way up through the ranks. She had taken on every task with dedication, proving herself time and time again.

Mrs Cartwright smiled warmly as Mary entered. "Mary, please sit down," she said, gesturing to a chair.

Mary sat, her hands clasped tightly in her lap. "You wanted to see me, Mrs Cartwright?"

"Yes, Mary. I have some good news for you," Mrs Cartwright began. "Your hard work and dedication have not gone unnoticed. Mr Everly and I have decided to promote you to the position of upstairs maid."

Mary's eyes widened, her heart soaring. "Upstairs maid? Really?"

Mrs Cartwright nodded. "Yes, you'll be responsible for cleaning and maintaining the bedrooms and other private areas of the house. It's a significant step up, and it comes with a pay raise."

Tears of joy filled Mary's eyes. "Thank you, Mrs Cartwright. Thank you so much. I promise I won't let you down."

"I'm sure you won't, Mary. You've earned this," Mrs Cartwright said. "You'll be working alongside a few of the older girls, and they'll help you get accustomed to your new duties."

Mary nodded eagerly, barely able to contain her happiness. "When do I start?"

"Tomorrow morning," Mrs Cartwright replied. "Take the rest of the day to prepare and rest, and be prepared for a long day tomorrow."

Mary thanked her profusely and left the parlour, her heart light and her steps quick. She felt as if she was walking on air. The promotion meant more money, and while she wasn't sure exactly what she was saving for, it felt good to have something to put aside for emergencies. Life had taught her to expect the unexpected, and she wanted to be prepared.

That evening, Mary sat on her small bed in the maids' quarters, staring at the small collection of coins she had saved. The promotion meant a significant increase in her wages, and she felt a surge of pride and security that she had never known before. She had worked tirelessly, and it was paying off.

Lizzie, now one of her closest friends, peeked into the room. "Mary, I heard the news! Congratulations!"

Mary beamed. "Thank you, Lizzie. I can hardly believe it. Upstairs maid!"

Lizzie sat beside her, giving her a warm hug. "You've earned it. No one works harder than you."

Mary smiled, feeling the warmth of Lizzie's words. "I'm just so happy. It's more money, and I can start saving properly. It feels good to have something set aside."

Lizzie nodded. "It's smart to save. You never know what life might throw at you. Tonight, let's just celebrate. We'll all be having a little gathering in the kitchen. You should join us."

Mary hesitated for a moment, then nodded. "I'd like that."

The celebration in the kitchen was lively. The other maids congratulated Mary, sharing stories and laughter late into the night. For the first time in a long while, Mary allowed herself to feel truly happy, surrounded by friends and a sense of accomplishment.

The next morning, Mary donned her new uniform with pride. The crisp black dress and white apron symbolised her new position. She stood before the mirror, smoothing out the fabric, her heart fluttering with a mix of excitement and nerves.

Mrs Cartwright greeted her with a nod of approval. "You look the part, Mary. Now, let's get started."

Mary followed Mrs Cartwright upstairs, her footsteps light on the polished wooden floors. The older girls, now her colleagues, welcomed her with smiles and guided her through her new responsibilities. She learned to dust and clean the intricate furniture, change the linens, and ensure the rooms were immaculate.

Rebecca, one of the older maids, showed Mary how to properly dust the ornate moulding in the drawing room. "You need to be gentle but thorough," she explained, her tone kind but professional. "The Everlys are very particular about their antiques."

Mary nodded, focusing intently on the task. "I understand. Thank you for showing me."

Rebecca smiled and patted her shoulder. "You'll do fine, Mary. Just take your time and don't rush. It's better to do it right the first time."

The work was harder than what Mary was used to, but she pushed through, determined to prove herself. She scrubbed floors until her knees ached, and carefully made the beds, ensuring every corner was perfectly tucked.

During supper, Mary found herself in the kitchen with the other maids. They chatted amongst themselves, their familiarity with each other evident. Mary felt a bit like an outsider, but she was grateful for their initial kindness.

Annie handed Mary a cup of tea. "Here, have this. You've been working hard."

"Thank you," Mary said, accepting the cup gratefully. "I'm just trying to keep up."

"You're doing great," Annie replied with a smile. "It's a lot to learn, but you'll get the hang of it. Just like you were great as a scullery maid when we first met."

Mary sipped her tea, the warmth spreading through her. "I appreciate that. I'm really grateful for this opportunity."

Lizzie joined them, wiping her hands on her apron. "You've got a good attitude, Mary. That's half the battle."

The other maids nodded in agreement, and Mary felt a small surge of hope. They were sweet, but a little distant, likely because they weren't used to having her upstairs just yet. She resolved to continue working hard and to earn their trust and friendship.

As the day wore on, Mary's muscles ached from the unfamiliar tasks, but she didn't let that slow her down. She focused on each job with precision, her mind set on doing everything to the best of her ability. The detailed work was challenging, but she found satisfaction in the meticulousness required.

By the time evening approached, Mary was exhausted but proud of what she had accomplished. Mrs Cartwright made a final inspection of the rooms, her keen eyes missing nothing.

"Well done, Mary," Mrs Cartwright said with a nod of approval. "Keep this up, Mr Everly has high standards, and I expect you to keep up this quality of work."

Mary beamed, the praise lifting her spirits. "Thank you, Mrs Cartwright. I'll keep working hard."

Chapter Eleven

Sunday morning dawned bright and clear, a rare day off for Mary. She dressed in her best clothes, a simple but neat dress, and joined Lizzie and Annie for the walk to church. The cobblestone streets were bustling with families heading in the same direction, their Sunday best on display.

The church, a grand Gothic structure with towering spires and stained glass windows, stood at the heart of the town. Mary felt a sense of peace wash over her as they entered, the familiar scent of polished wood and burning candles filling the air. The congregation was already gathering, and the sound of the organ playing softly in the background added to the reverent atmosphere.

They found seats near the middle, and Mary settled in, glancing around at the familiar faces of the townsfolk. The service began with the vicar leading the congregation in a hymn, the rich voices rising to the rafters.

Mary joined in, her voice blending with the others. She had always found solace in these moments, the hymns a reminder of the constancy of faith amidst the uncertainties of life.

After the hymn, the vicar read from the Book of Common Prayer, his voice steady and authoritative. "Dearly beloved, we are gathered here in the sight of God, to offer up our praises and thanksgivings for the manifold blessings which we daily receive at His hands, to set forth His most worthy praise, to hear His most holy Word, and to ask those things which are requisite and necessary, as well for the body as the soul."

Mary listened intently, finding comfort in the familiar words. The service proceeded with prayers and readings from the Bible, the congregation participating in the liturgy with practiced ease.

The sermon followed, the vicar speaking about the importance of faith and community. He emphasised the need to support one another, especially in times of hardship. Mary found herself reflecting on her own journey, the struggles she had faced, and the support she had found in unexpected places.

As the service drew to a close, the congregation stood for the final hymn.

The hymn ended, and the vicar gave the benediction. "The grace of our Lord Jesus Christ, and the love of God, and the fellowship of the Holy Ghost, be with us all evermore. Amen."

With the service concluded, the congregation slowly filtered out of the church, gathering in small groups to chat and catch up. Mary stood with Lizzie and Annie, enjoying the warmth of the sun and the pleasant hum of conversation around them.

As they chatted, the vicar approached, accompanied by a young man Mary had not seen before. The vicar smiled warmly. "Good morning, ladies. May I introduce you to Mr John Bradshaw, our new assistant curate?"

John Bradshaw stepped forward, a pleasant smile on his face. He was a tall, handsome young man with kind eyes and an air of quiet confidence. "It's a pleasure to meet you all," he said, his voice gentle but firm.

Lizzie and Annie greeted him warmly, and Mary found herself captivated by his presence. "Welcome, Mr Bradshaw," she said, extending her hand. "I'm Mary Beckwith."

He shook her hand, his grip firm but gentle. "Thank you, Miss Beckwith. It's a pleasure to be here. I've heard many good things about this community."

The vicar nodded. "Mr Bradshaw will be assisting with the services and helping with the various charitable works of the church. I'm introducing him to our church members. I'm sure you'll all get to know him well."

As they chatted, Mary felt a spark of curiosity and interest. John Bradshaw seemed genuinely kind and dedicated to his work. She couldn't help but wonder what his story was and how he had come to their town.

After a while, the vicar and Mr Bradshaw moved on to greet other members of the congregation. Lizzie nudged Mary playfully. "Looks like we've got a new face around here. What do you think?"

Mary smiled, a little flustered. "He seems nice. It will be interesting to see what he brings to the community."

Annie grinned. "He does have a certain charm, doesn't he? Maybe he'll make things a bit more lively around here."

They laughed together, the camaraderie and shared humour making Mary feel even more at home. As they walked back to the townhouse, Mary's thoughts kept drifting back to the new assistant curate. She couldn't shake the feeling that his arrival marked the beginning of something new, a subtle shift in the fabric of her life that she couldn't quite define.

Chapter Twelve

Over the next three months, Mary saw John Bradshaw frequently, both at church services and around town as he went about his duties. As the weather grew colder and winter approached, she found herself looking forward to Sundays more than ever. There was something about his presence that brought warmth to the coldest days.

One Sunday, Mary and Annie sat in their usual spot with Lizzie, waiting for the service to begin. The church was bustling with the sounds of people settling in, and the scent of burning candles filled the air.

Annie nudged Mary, grinning. "Did you hear about old Mrs Maxwell's cat?

Apparently, it climbed up the vicar's tree and refused to come down."

Mary laughed, imagining the scene. "Oh dear, I hope the vicar didn't have to climb up after it!"

Lizzie shook her head, chuckling. "No, he sent young Timmy up instead. Poor lad looked terrified."

They all laughed; the sound blending with the murmurs of the congregation. As the laughter died down, Annie noticed Mary's gaze drifting across the church. Following her line of sight, she saw Mary's eyes lingering on John Bradshaw, who was talking to a few parishioners near the front.

Annie smirked and nudged Lizzie, whispering loudly enough for Mary to hear.

"Look who's got her eye on the new assistant curate!"

Mary's cheeks flushed a deep red, and she quickly looked away. "I wasn't staring," she protested weakly.

Lizzie raised an eyebrow, a teasing smile on her lips. "Oh, really? Because it looked like you were practically burning a hole in the back of his head."

Annie giggled. "Admit it, Mary. You like him."

Mary tried to maintain her composure, but the heat in her cheeks betrayed her. "I just think he's... interesting. That's all."

Lizzie leaned in, her voice conspiratorial. "Interesting, hmm? What exactly do you find interesting about him?"

Mary fumbled for words, her embarrassment making it difficult to think straight. "Well, he's kind to us even though we're below his station, and he seems genuinely dedicated to helping people. He's always so calm and composed."

Annie grinned. "He's handsome. Don't forget handsome."

Mary's blush deepened, and she couldn't help but laugh at herself. "All right, fine. He *is* handsome. Happy now?"

Lizzie and Annie exchanged triumphant looks, satisfied with Mary's reluctant confession. "Very happy," Annie said, still giggling. "You know, there's no harm in looking, Mary."

Before Mary could respond, the organ began to play, signalling the start of the service. The congregation rose to their feet, and the vicar, followed by John Bradshaw, walked to the front of the church. Mary's heart fluttered as she stole one last glance at him, then quickly focused on her hymn book.

The opening hymn filled the church, the rich voices of the congregation rising to the rafters.

As the service proceeded, Mary tried to keep her thoughts on the prayers and readings, but she couldn't help the occasional glance in John's direction. He stood with a quiet dignity, his presence a steadying influence on those around him.

When the vicar began his sermon, Mary forced herself to pay attention. He spoke about the importance of faith and perseverance, especially as the winter months approached and challenges became more difficult. His words resonated with Mary, reminding her of the strength she had found within herself over the years.

Even as she listened, her thoughts kept drifting back to John Bradshaw. There was something about him that captivated her, something that made her feel hopeful in a way she hadn't felt in a long time.

As the service drew to a close and the final hymn began, Mary joined in with renewed spirit.

The hymn ended, and the vicar gave the benediction. "The grace of our Lord Jesus Christ, and the love of God, and the fellowship of the Holy Ghost, be with us all evermore. Amen."

With the service concluded, the congregation began to file out of the church. Mary, Annie, and Lizzie lingered for a moment, chatting quietly as they gathered their things.

As they stepped outside into the crisp winter air, Annie and Lizzie walked ahead, still joking and laughing about the service and the latest gossip in town. Mary followed a few steps behind, her thoughts drifting back to John Bradshaw. She watched him as he mingled with the parishioners, his kind smile and gentle demeanour putting everyone at ease.

Annie turned back to Mary, grinning. "Come on, Mary! You're lagging behind. Daydreaming about Mr Bradshaw again?"

Mary forced a smile and quickened her pace to catch up. "I'm coming, I'm coming. Just lost in thought, that's all."

Lizzie gave her a knowing look. "Lost in thoughts of a certain assistant curate, perhaps?"

Mary laughed, trying to brush off their teasing. "You two are impossible. Let's just enjoy the walk, shall we?"

As they made their way through the bustling streets, the cold air nipping at their cheeks, Mary's mind wandered. She knew deep down that nothing could ever happen between her and John Bradshaw. He was so far above her station, a respected member of the church community, and she was just a maid. Moreover, he was older than her and burdened with many responsibilities that she couldn't begin to understand.

Annie and Lizzie continued their playful banter, their laughter echoing off the buildings as they walked ahead. Mary tried to join in, but her heart wasn't fully in it. She glanced back at the church, where John was still speaking with the vicar. She sighed, a mixture of longing and resignation settling in her chest.

"You all right, Mary?" Annie asked, noticing her friend's pensive expression.

Mary nodded, forcing another smile. "Yes, just thinking about everything I have to do at the house tomorrow. You know how busy it gets during the holidays."

Lizzie linked her arm through Mary's. "Don't worry, we'll get through it together. Besides, it's our day off. Let's not think about work just yet."

Mary appreciated their efforts to cheer her up, and she allowed herself to be drawn into their conversation. They talked about the upcoming Christmas preparations, the decorations they had seen around town, and the festive foods they hoped to enjoy. For a little while, Mary managed to push aside her thoughts of John and focus on the simple joys of the season.

As they approached the townhouse, the three girls paused to say their goodbyes. Annie and Lizzie were planning to meet up later for some Christmas shopping, but Mary decided to spend the rest of her day off quietly at home.

"Are you sure you don't want to come with us?" Annie asked. "It could be fun."

Mary shook her head with a gentle smile. "Thank you, but I think I'll stay in today. Enjoy your shopping, and I'll see you both tomorrow."

Lizzie gave her a quick hug. "All right, but don't stay cooped up inside all day. We'll see you tomorrow."

Mary waved them off and walked up the steps to the townhouse. As she entered the warmth of the house, she let out a long breath. The familiar scent of freshly baked bread and the comforting hum of the household activities enveloped her.

She made her way to her small room and sat by the window, gazing out at the snow-covered streets. Her thoughts drifted back to John Bradshaw, and she allowed herself a moment to daydream about what could never be. She imagined talking to him, sharing stories, and maybe even laughing together as they walked through the town.

Reality quickly set in. She knew that such dreams were just that—dreams. John Bradshaw had his life, his duties, and his place in the world. She had hers. It was enough to admire him from afar and to find joy in the simple act of seeing him each Sunday.

Chapter Thirteen

A few weeks later, snow blanketed the town, transforming it into a picturesque winter wonderland. The cold air nipped at Mary's cheeks as she hurried to church with Annie and Lizzie, her thoughts focused on the busy morning ahead. She had a lot of work waiting for her at the Everly townhouse, and she wanted to rush home after the service to prepare for the day.

As they entered the church, Mary noticed a sense of excitement and anticipation among the congregation. She glanced at Annie and Lizzie, who shrugged, equally curious. They found their usual seats, and

Mary settled in, hoping the service would be brief.

The organ began to play, and the congregation stood for the opening hymn. The familiar melody filled the church, and Mary found herself momentarily lost in the music.

When the hymn ended, the vicar stepped forward, his expression serious. "Before we begin our service today, we have an important announcement."

Mary's heart skipped a beat, sensing that something significant was about to be said. She glanced at John Bradshaw, who stood beside the vicar, his face composed but with a hint of something she couldn't quite place.

The vicar nodded to John, who stepped forward. "Good morning, everyone," he began, his voice steady and calm. "I have been with this parish for several months now, and it has been a blessing to serve such a wonderful community."

A murmur of agreement rippled through the congregation, and Mary felt her pulse quicken. She had a sinking feeling she knew what was coming.

John continued, "I wanted to let you all know that I have been offered a position as the vicar of my own church, and I have decided to accept it. I will be leaving this parish after Christmas to begin my new role."

Mary felt as if the ground had shifted beneath her feet. Her heart sank, and a wave of sadness washed over her. She had known that nothing could happen between them, but the thought of not seeing him every Sunday was unexpectedly painful.

Annie noticed Mary's reaction and placed a comforting hand on her arm. "Mary, are you all right?"

Mary nodded, but she couldn't hide the tears that welled up in her eyes. "I'm fine," she whispered, her voice trembling.

Lizzie, usually quick with a joke, saw Mary's distress and remained silent, offering a supportive presence instead. The rest of the congregation seemed to blur around Mary as she struggled to process the news.

John continued, "I want to thank you all for your kindness and support during my time here. It has meant more to me than words can express. I will carry the memories of this parish with me always."

The vicar took over again, leading the congregation in a prayer for John's success in his new role. Mary bowed her head, but her thoughts were a jumble of emotions. She had admired John from afar, finding solace and hope in his presence. His departure felt like the loss of a dream, however unattainable it had been.

As the service continued, Mary struggled to focus on the prayers and hymns. Her mind kept drifting back to John's announcement, the sadness settling heavily in her heart. When the final hymn ended and the congregation began to file out, Mary lingered, not wanting to face the cold reality outside.

Annie and Lizzie waited with her, their usual chatter subdued. "I'm so sorry, Mary," Annie said softly. "I know how much you admired him."

Mary managed a weak smile. "Thank you, Annie. I'll be all right. It's just…unexpected."

Lizzie gave her a reassuring hug. "We should be happy for him."

"I am happy for him. Truly. It's a wonderful opportunity…"

"You're still disappointed, though. I understand."

Mary nodded, appreciating their support but feeling the weight of her disappointment. As they stepped outside into the falling snow, she couldn't help but glance back at the church, feeling a sense of loss.

As they walked down the steps, Mary saw John Bradshaw approaching them. He waved and quickened his pace, his breath visible in the cold air. "Good morning, ladies," he greeted warmly, his eyes twinkling with his usual kindness.

"Good morning, Mr Bradshaw," Annie and Lizzie chorused, smiling.

John's gaze settled on Mary, who did her best to maintain her composure. "I wanted to thank you all for being such a wonderful part of this parish. I've enjoyed my time here immensely," he said. "I just hope nobody will miss me terribly." He chuckled, but Mary could only manage a weak smile.

"We'll definitely miss you," Lizzie said honestly, glancing at Mary.

"Yes, it won't be the same without you," Annie added, nudging Mary gently.

Mary swallowed hard, trying to keep her emotions in check. "We'll miss you, Mr Bradshaw. You've been a wonderful addition to the parish."

John smiled, but there was a hint of sadness in his eyes. "Thank you, Mary. That means a lot to me. I'm sure you all will continue to thrive here. This is a strong community."

Mary nodded, her heart heavy with the knowledge that this would be one of their last conversations. "We wish you all the best in your new role. They're lucky to have you."

John's expression softened. "Thank you, Mary. That means more than you know." He paused, looking around at the snow-covered street and the bustling townspeople. "I've learned so much here and met so many wonderful people. It's going to be hard to leave."

Mary's throat tightened, but she forced herself to keep her voice steady. "We're grateful for everything you've done. You've made a real difference."

John gave her a warm smile, then turned to Annie and Lizzie. "Take care, all of you. I'm sure we'll see each other again before I leave, but I wanted to make sure you knew how much I appreciate your kindness and support."

With a final nod, John walked away, his figure gradually blending into the crowd. Mary watched him go, her heart aching with a mix of admiration and sorrow.

Annie looped her arm through Mary's. "Come on, Mary. Let's head home."

Lizzie walked on Mary's other side, her presence comforting. "We'll get through this together, all right?"

Mary nodded, grateful for their friendship. "All right," she said softly, trying to summon a smile.

As they made their way back to the townhouse, the snow continued to fall gently around them, a silent witness to the changes in Mary's heart. She knew she had to be strong, to keep moving forward despite the disappointment. The support of her friends and the memories of John's kindness would help her face whatever came next.

Chapter Fourteen

It had been a year since John left the parish, and as Christmas approached, Mary found herself feeling increasingly melancholic. The festive season, which brought so much joy to others, only seemed to highlight the void in her life. She watched as townsfolk bustled about, their laughter and cheer filling the air as they moved from shop to shop, buying gifts and treats for the holiday.

For Mary, the holiday season was a stark reminder of her loneliness.

Each day, she walked the snow-covered streets, observing the cheerful faces around her. Families huddled together, children dragging their parents towards brightly decorated windows, and couples walked hand in hand, sharing whispered secrets and stolen kisses. Mary had no one special to give a present to, no one special to share any of the simple joys of the season. Her family was gone, and the one person she longed to see most, John Bradshaw, was nowhere to be found.

Mary's routine at the Everly townhouse provided some distraction. The household was a flurry of activity as they prepared for the numerous holiday guests. She threw herself into her work, finding solace in the busyness. The familiar tasks kept her hands and mind occupied, but her heart remained heavy.

One evening, as she started another task, Mary overheard Lizzie and Annie talking excitedly about their plans for Christmas. Lizzie was looking forward to a visit from her family, while Annie couldn't wait to see her young nieces and nephews.

"Are you doing anything special for Christmas, Mary?" Annie asked, her eyes bright with curiosity.

Mary forced a smile. "No, nothing special. Just the usual work around here; but it's all right. I enjoy the holiday preparations."

Lizzie gave her a sympathetic look. "You should take some time for yourself, Mary. You work so hard."

Mary shrugged, trying to keep her tone light. "I don't mind. It keeps me busy."

The conversation moved on, but Mary's thoughts lingered on the emptiness of her own holiday plans. She couldn't help but think of John, wondering where he was and how he was spending his Christmas. She missed his presence, his kindness, and the way he made her feel seen and valued.

***

One particularly cold evening, as she walked home from the market, Mary passed by a group of carollers singing joyfully in the town square. Their voices rang out through the crisp air, and the sight of them brought tears to her eyes. She paused, listening to the familiar carols, the melodies stirring memories of happier times.

The words echoed in her mind, and Mary felt a pang of longing. She wished she could share this moment with someone special, someone who understood her heart. She wished she could share it with John.

As the days passed, Mary's spirits remained low. The town was ablaze with lights and decorations, but the festive atmosphere only deepened her sense of isolation. She tried to stay cheerful for the sake of her friends but it was an effort to keep up the facade.

On Christmas Eve, the Everly household was in full swing, hosting a grand party for their guests. Mary and the other maids worked tirelessly, ensuring everything ran smoothly. The sound of laughter and music filled the air, and the guests revelled in the festive spirit.

She caught glimpses of the guests, their faces alight with joy, and felt a pang of envy.

She longed for that kind of happiness, the kind that seemed to come so easily to others.

As the evening wore on, Mary found a moment to herself in the kitchen. She leaned against the counter, taking a deep breath to steady her emotions. The warmth of the kitchen contrasted sharply with the cold outside, but it did little to ease the chill in her heart.

Lizzie entered, carrying a tray of empty glasses. She saw Mary and gave her a concerned look. "Are you okay, Mary? You seem a bit down."

Mary nodded, forcing a smile. "I'm fine, Lizzie. Just tired, I suppose. It's been a long day."

Lizzie set down the tray and walked over to her. "You know, it's okay to feel sad sometimes. Especially during the holidays. We all miss people we've lost."

Mary looked down, her eyes glistening with unshed tears. "I know. It's just... hard. Especially this time of year."

Lizzie hugged her gently. "You're not alone, Mary. We're here for you. Things will get better. I promise."

Mary hugged her back, grateful for her friend's kindness. "Thank you, Lizzie. That means a lot."

The night eventually came to an end, and the guests departed, leaving the house quiet once more. Mary finished her tasks and retired to her small room, feeling the weight of her loneliness more acutely than ever. She lay in bed, staring at the ceiling, thinking of John and wondering if he ever thought of her.

Christmas Day came and went, another day filled with heartache for Mary. She missed her mother and father, and John. She briefly thought about asking the vicar where John had gone at Christmas service, but knew it would do her no good. He wouldn't want a lowly maid. And she vowed to forget him, even though the ache in her heart told her it would not be easy to do.

Chapter Fifteen

One year later

The first week of December arrived, and with it came the flurry of activity as Mary and the other maids prepared the Everly household for the grand Christmas party. This year's party was to be the biggest yet, a festive tradition that the Everlys held every December.

Mary, Annie, Lizzie, and the other maids worked tirelessly, their hands busy and their hearts light with anticipation. The house was to be transformed into a winter wonderland, and the preparations required meticulous attention to detail.

Mary stood on a small ladder, carefully hanging sprigs of holly and pine boughs above the doors and windows. The scent of the fresh greenery filled the air, mingling with the crisp, cold breeze that wafted in whenever the door opened.

"Careful, Mary," Annie called from below, holding the ladder steady. "We don't need you falling and breaking something days before the party."

Mary laughed, adjusting the bough she was placing. "Don't worry, Annie, I'm fine."

Lizzie was wrapping red and green ribbons around the balustrades along the stairs and balconies, her nimble fingers working quickly. "Just wait until you see the whole place lit up. It's going to be magical," she said, a sparkle of excitement in her eyes.

Mary climbed down from the ladder and helped place bunches of white candles throughout the house, even though it wasn't necessary for illumination since the residence had gas lighting. The candles added a touch of old-world charm and a soft, warm glow that gas lights couldn't replicate.

"I love how the candles make everything feel so cosy," Mary said, carefully positioning a candle on a side table.

"It does make the place feel special," Lizzie agreed, tying a final ribbon around the banister. "The guests always love it."

As they worked, laughter and chatter filled the house. The maids shared stories and jokes, their camaraderie lifting their spirits as they transformed the residence. Despite the hard work, the festive atmosphere made the tasks enjoyable.

Annie held up a piece of mistletoe, a mischievous grin spreading across her face. "Where do you think we should put this?"

Lizzie rolled her eyes but smiled. "Somewhere out of sight. We don't need the guests getting carried away."

Mary giggled. "Or maybe right in the middle of the ballroom, just to see what happens."

The laughter that followed was infectious, and even Mrs Cartwright couldn't help but smile as she passed by. "All right, ladies, keep up the good work. We still have a lot to do over the next several days."

***

The maids continued their tasks with renewed vigour as the day of the party drew near. They hung wreaths on the doors and windows, strung garlands along the walls, and set the tables with the finest china and silverware. The grand Christmas tree, adorned with twinkling lights and glittering ornaments, stood proudly in the centre of the ballroom.

Mary took a step back, admiring their handiwork. The house looked enchanting, every corner filled with holiday cheer. She felt a pang of sadness, knowing she had no one special to share this moment with, but the joy of the season and the warmth of her friends' laughter helped to ease the loneliness.

As the day wore on and the final touches were added, the Everly household began to buzz with anticipation. Tomorrow was the party. Although it was always hard work, Mary enjoyed mingling with the maids and savouring the delicious food that was set aside for them. The master and mistress of the house, Mr and Mrs Everly, inspected the decorations and nodded approvingly.

"You've all done a splendid job," Mrs Everly said, her eyes shining with pride. "This will be a Christmas party to remember."

Mary smiled, feeling a sense of accomplishment. Despite the hard work and the lingering sadness in her heart, she was proud of what they had achieved. The house was ready to welcome its guests, and the spirit of Christmas filled the air. But Mary could not feel the happiness and peace she so desired.

Chapter Sixteen

On the day of the party, the Everly household was a whirlwind of activity. Mary and the other maids were busy from dawn until dusk, ensuring everything was perfect for the evening's festivities. The grand house needed to sparkle, and there were countless tasks to complete.

Mary started her day in the kitchen, helping to prepare the vast array of dishes that would be served. The scent of roasting meats and baking pies filled the air, mingling with the fresh pine from the garlands they had hung. Annie and Lizzie were polishing the silverware and setting the tables with the finest china.

"Make sure those glasses are spotless," Mrs Cartwright instructed as she passed by, her keen eyes missing nothing. "The guests will be arriving soon."

Mary nodded, focusing on her task. She moved efficiently, washing, drying, and placing each glass with care. Once the kitchen duties were complete, she joined the others in the hallways, ensuring every surface was dust-free and every decoration perfectly in place.

As the sun set and the guests began to arrive, the maids were instructed to stay out of sight, maintaining the background work that kept the party running smoothly. They refilled drinks, replaced empty plates, and quietly moved through the house, their presence nearly invisible.

Mary found herself in a quiet corner of the hallway, refilling a tray of glasses. The sound of music and laughter drifted through the open doors, drawing her attention. She peered cautiously around the corner, curious but mindful of her duties.

In the grand ballroom, Mr and Mrs Everly were dancing gracefully across the floor. Mrs Everly's gown shimmered pink in the candlelight, and Mr Everly looked dashing in his tailored suit. They moved in perfect harmony, their smiles radiant and their eyes only for each other.

Mary's heart ached with a familiar longing as she watched them. She wished she had someone to dance with like that; someone who would look at her the way Mr Everly looked at his wife. The thought of John

Bradshaw crossed her mind, and she quickly pushed it away, not wanting to dampen the moment with sadness.

She was so absorbed in her thoughts that she didn't notice Mrs Cartwright approaching. "Mary, what are you doing here?" she whispered sharply, startling Mary out of her reverie.

"I'm sorry, Mrs Cartwright," Mary replied, stepping back quickly. "I was just—"

"Get back to work, girl. We have a party to run," Mrs Cartwright said.

Mary nodded, her heart still aching from the glimpse of the Everlys dancing. She turned and made her way back to her duties, pushing her own longings aside. There were still many tasks to complete, and she couldn't afford to be distracted.

As she moved through the hallway, ensuring everything was in order, she heard footsteps behind her. She turned to see a male guest, clearly drunk, stumbling towards her. His clothes were dishevelled, and his eyes were glassy.

"Excuse me, sir," Mary said politely, "the ballroom is that way." She pointed in the direction of the festivities, hoping he would take the hint and leave her alone.

The man smiled, but it wasn't a friendly smile. "I'm not looking to dance," he slurred, stepping closer.

Mary's heart pounded in her chest. She tried to back away, keeping her voice calm.

"Perhaps you should return to the party, sir. It's not safe to wander the house alone."

He ignored her suggestion, his gaze fixed on her. "What's your name, girl?"

"Mary," she replied, glancing around for any sign of help. The hallway was empty, and the sounds of the party were distant.

"Mary," he repeated, as if savouring the word. "Pretty name for a pretty girl."

Mary took another step back, but the man moved closer, cornering her against the wall. "Please, sir, I have work to do," she said, her voice trembling.

He chuckled, his breath reeking of alcohol. "Work can wait. Let's have a little chat."

Mary's mind raced as she tried to think of a way to escape. She attempted to step around him, but he grabbed her wrist, pulling her closer. "You're a feisty one, aren't you?"

"Let me go," Mary insisted, trying to pull her hand free, but his grip tightened.

"Why so nervous, Mary?" he said, his voice dripping with mock concern. "I'm just trying to be friendly."

Mary's heart pounded in her chest as she struggled against his hold. "Please, let me go."

Ignoring her pleas, he leaned in, his face inches from hers. "I think you need to learn to relax," he murmured, his grip like a vice.

Mary felt a surge of panic as he tried to kiss her. She pushed against him with all her strength, wanting to scream but holding it in. Summoning all her courage, she managed to push him away, but he quickly grabbed her again, pulling her closer.

Desperate, Mary scratched his face, her nails leaving deep marks on his cheek. Taking advantage of his momentary shock, she darted around the corner, her heart pounding in her chest. She nearly collided with Mrs Everly, who was walking down the hallway.

"Mary! What on earth—" Mrs Everly began, but before Mary could explain, the man stumbled around the corner, his face red with anger and marked by fresh scratches.

"This little wench attacked me!" he shouted, pointing an accusing finger at Mary. "Look what she did to my face!"

Mrs Everly's eyes widened in shock and outrage as she turned to Mary. "Is this true? Did you hurt one of our guests?"

"No, Mrs Everly," Mary said, her voice trembling. "He tried to—he grabbed me and tried to kiss me. I was just trying to defend myself."

Mrs Everly's face hardened. "How dare you lie! Our guests are to be treated with the utmost respect. You've brought shame upon this household."

"Mrs Everly, he—" Mary tried to protest, but Mrs Everly cut her off.

"Enough! I won't hear another word," Mrs Everly snapped. She grabbed Mary by the arm, her grip firm and unyielding. "You will come with me to the study. This behaviour will not go unpunished."

Tears welled up in Mary's eyes as she was dragged down the hallway, the festive decorations and laughter from the ballroom now a distant, cruel mockery of the night's earlier warmth. Her heart sank, knowing that no one would believe her side of the story. As they reached the study, Mrs Everly opened the door and pushed Mary inside, her face a mask of fury and disappointment.

Mary stood in the study, her heart racing, as Mrs Everly's eyes blazed with fury. The lavishly decorated room, with its mahogany furniture and richly patterned rugs, seemed to close in on her, making it hard to breathe. She could hear the muffled sounds of the party continuing outside the door, a stark contrast to the tension-filled silence within.

Mrs Everly took a deep breath and began her tirade. "Mary, I am utterly disappointed in you. This behaviour is beyond unacceptable. My husband and I have been nothing but generous to you. We allowed you to work here when you had nowhere else to go. We kept you on despite your background, and what do we get in return? This!"

Mary tried to speak, but Mrs Everly held up a hand to silence her. "Do you have any idea what you've done tonight? You've assaulted a guest in our home! A man of good standing and reputation, and you think you can just scratch his face and run away?"

"Mrs Everly," Mary said, her voice trembling, "he cornered me and—"

"Enough!" Mrs Everly snapped, her voice cutting through Mary's words like a knife. "I will not tolerate lies and disrespect under my roof. After all we've done for you, you repay us with deceit and violence. How dare you!"

Tears streamed down Mary's face as she tried to find the words to defend herself. "Please, Mrs Everly, you must believe me. He—"

"I said enough!" Mrs Everly's voice rose, her face flushing with anger. "Do you think I care for your excuses? My husband and I have provided you with a home, food, a steady job. We even promoted you twice! And this is how you repay our kindness?"

Mary's mind flashed back to the years she had spent working diligently in the Everly household, her dedication and hard work earning her those promotions. She had always been grateful for the opportunities she had been given, and the thought of losing everything because of one man's actions filled her with despair.

"Mrs Everly, I swear I'm telling the truth," Mary pleaded, her voice cracking. "He was drunk and he tried to force himself on me. I didn't mean to hurt him, I was just trying to get away."

Mrs Everly's eyes narrowed, her expression hardening further. "You have brought disgrace to this household. My husband will not take this lightly. Just wait until I tell him what you've done."

With that, she turned sharply and left the room, leaving Mary standing there, shaking and overwhelmed with fear. Mary could hear the sound of her footsteps fading down the hallway, the heavy weight of impending judgment settling in her chest.

Mary looked around the room, her eyes landing on the family portraits that adorned the walls. The smiling faces of the Everly family seemed to mock her, a painful reminder of the gap between her own station and theirs. She thought of all the nights she had spent working late, the early mornings, the countless hours of effort she had put into her job. It had all led to this moment, where everything hung in the balance.

Minutes felt like hours as she stood there, waiting for the inevitable. She could hear muffled voices outside the door, the sound of the party continuing as if nothing had happened. She wondered what the other maids would think, if they would believe her or side with Mrs Everly. She knew that in the eyes of the upper class, a maid's word would always be doubted, especially against that of a guest.

The door suddenly swung open, and Mrs Everly returned, her husband, Mr Everly, by her side. His face was stern, his expression one of barely contained anger. Mary's heart sank further, knowing that her fate now rested in his hands.

"What's this I hear about you attacking one of my guests?" Mr Everly demanded, his voice cold and authoritative.

Mary opened her mouth to speak, but Mrs Everly cut in. "She scratched his face, William! I found her running away, and she had the audacity to lie to me about what happened. This is how she repays us after all these years of kindness and trust."

Mr Everly turned his piercing gaze on Mary. "Explain yourself."

Mary took a deep breath, trying to steady her voice. "Sir, he was drunk and cornered me in the hallway. He forced himself on me, and I only scratched him to get away. I promise you, I wasn't trying to cause trouble. I was just defending myself."

Mr Everly's eyes narrowed, his jaw clenched. He glanced at his wife, who shook her head vehemently. "I don't know what to believe, Mary," he said finally. "I cannot have my household tarnished by such behaviour. We need to maintain our reputation."

Mrs Everly stepped forward, her voice dripping with disdain. "William, she has proven she cannot be trusted. We cannot allow this to go unpunished."

Mr Everly nodded slowly, his decision made. "Very well. Mary. We have no choice but to let you go."

Chapter Seventeen

The next morning, Mary was awakened by the harsh knock on the door of the maid's quarters. She rubbed her eyes, still red from crying, and opened the door to find Mr Everly standing there, his face a mask of cold indifference.

"Get your things," he said curtly. "You're leaving."

"Mr Everly, please," Mary began, her voice trembling. "I've worked here for years. Please, let me explain—"

"There is nothing more to explain," he interrupted, his tone icy. "Your behaviour last night was disgraceful. You assaulted a guest and brought shame upon this household. You will leave immediately."

Mary's heart sank as she hurriedly gathered her few belongings. She wanted to say goodbye to Lizzie and Annie, to explain what had happened, but she knew there was no time. They slept in another room and would not be awake for another half an hour or more. Tears blurred her vision as she threw her belongings into a small bag.

When she emerged from her room, Mr Everly was waiting, his expression unyielding. "Let's go," he said, leading her to the front door. The house was still and silent, the early morning light casting long shadows across the floor. The festive decorations that had seemed so cheerful now felt like a cruel mockery of her situation.

As they reached the front door, Mary turned to Mr Everly, desperation in her voice. "Please, Mr Everly, I have nowhere to go. It's so close to Christmas, and it's cold. Please, give me a chance to explain to Lizzie and Annie. They'll vouch for me."

Mr Everly's face remained impassive. "This is not my concern. You have brought this upon yourself."

"Where will I go? How will I survive?" Mary pleaded, her voice breaking.

"I don't care," he replied bluntly. "You are no longer our concern."

With that, he opened the door and pushed her out into the cold morning. Mary stumbled into the snow, the biting wind cutting through her thin coat. She turned back, hoping for some sign of compassion, but Mr Everly had already closed the door.

Shivering, Mary clutched her bag and started walking. The snow was falling steadily, the streets covered in a thick blanket of white. She made her way to the inn where she had seen travellers coming and going, hoping to find shelter. But as she approached, she saw the innkeeper shaking his head.

"I'm sorry, miss," he said, his voice kind but firm. "We're filled up with Christmas visitors. There's no room."

Mary nodded numbly, her heart sinking further. She turned and headed to a nearby boarding house, praying they might have space for her. She knocked on the door, and a middle-aged woman answered, her face lined with worry.

"Can I help you?" the woman asked.

"Please," Mary said, her voice trembling. "I need a place to stay. Just for a few nights. I can work to pay my way."

The woman shook her head slowly. "I'm sorry, dear, but we're full. We've taken in as many as we can. I wish I could help."

Mary thanked her and turned away, her tears mingling with the snowflakes on her cheeks. She walked aimlessly through the town, the cold seeping into her bones. The festive lights and decorations only deepened her sense of despair. Families and couples walked past her, their laughter and joy a stark contrast to her loneliness and fear.

As the sky darkened, Mary's desperation grew. She had no idea where she would spend the night, and the bitter cold was becoming unbearable. She hurried down the street, her footsteps quickening as the shadows lengthened. The wind howled around her, and she pulled her coat tighter, though it did little to keep the cold at bay.

She thought of the warmth and safety of the Everly household, the laughter of Lizzie and Annie, and the sense of belonging she had felt there. Now, all of that was gone, and she was alone in the world, with no one to turn to.

Mary's thoughts raced as she walked, her mind filled with fear of what would happen if she stopped. She had heard stories of people freezing to death on cold nights like this, their bodies found stiff and lifeless in the morning. She couldn't let that happen to her.

She had to keep moving, had to find shelter somehow.

As the night deepened, Mary's steps faltered. She was exhausted, her body numb with cold. She looked around, hoping to find some place, any place, to rest. The town seemed empty, the streets deserted as people huddled in their warm homes, celebrating the season.

With a final burst of determination, Mary pushed on, her eyes scanning the darkening street. She didn't know where she was going, but she couldn't afford to stop. Not yet. Not until she found somewhere safe.

Her breath came in ragged gasps, the cold air burning her lungs. She stumbled forward, driven by the sheer will to survive, hoping against hope that she would find shelter before it was too late.

Mary hurried through the snow-covered streets, her heart pounding as she desperately searched for shelter. The sky had turned a deep, foreboding grey, and the biting wind cut through her thin coat. The festive decorations and cheerful lights of the town seemed to mock her as she trudged on, her steps growing heavier with each passing moment.

As she passed an inn, the sound of raucous laughter reached her ears. She glanced over and saw two men stumble out, clearly drunk. They spotted her immediately, their eyes narrowing as they called out.

"Hey there, little lady!" one of them slurred, his voice carrying through the night. "Where you off to in such a hurry?"

Mary's heart raced, a wave of panic washing over her. She quickened her pace, head down, trying to ignore them. Memories of the man's attempted kiss at the Everly townhouse, his burning grasp on her wrist, flashed through her mind. She couldn't let that happen again.

"Oi! We're talking to you!" the other man shouted, stumbling after her.

Fear propelled her forward, her footsteps quickening as she fled down the street. The laughter and shouts faded behind her, but the fear remained, gnawing at her insides. The darkness closed in around her, the cold seeping into her bones.

The streets grew quieter as the night deepened, the rowdy inns giving way to darkened shops and silent houses. Mary's exhaustion was beginning to overtake her, each step requiring more effort than the last. She wrapped her arms tightly around herself, trying to conserve what little warmth she had left.

Her mind raced with fear and desperation. She had nowhere to go, no one to turn to. Every door she had knocked on had been closed to her. The wind howled around her, and the snow fell in thick, heavy flakes, coating everything in a blanket of white.

She stumbled past another darkened inn, the sound of laughter and music faintly audible through the thick walls. She couldn't stop, couldn't risk encountering more drunkards. She had to keep moving, had to find somewhere safe.

Her strength was waning. Her legs felt like lead, her breath coming in short, painful gasps. She looked around, hoping to find some place, any place, where she could rest. The town seemed to stretch on endlessly, the darkened streets offering no refuge.

Her vision blurred with tears and exhaustion, and she tripped over a loose cobblestone, falling to her knees in the snow. She forced herself to stand, her entire body trembling with cold and fatigue. She had to keep going.

As she walked, the buildings became more and more dilapidated, the signs of life fading away. The once bustling town now seemed abandoned, the windows of the buildings boarded up, the doors locked tight.

Mary's hope was dwindling, her exhaustion overtaking her. She could barely lift her feet, each step a monumental effort. She looked around, her eyes desperate, and spotted an old, abandoned building, its doorway partially sheltered from the wind.

With the last of her strength, she stumbled towards it, collapsing into the doorway. The cold, hard stone pressed against her back as she huddled there, trying to shield herself from the biting wind.

Her breath came in ragged gasps, her body numb with cold. She hugged her knees to her chest, tears streaming down her face. She had nowhere to go, no one to help her. The darkness closed in, and she felt herself slipping into unconsciousness, her mind drifting in and out of awareness.

The sounds of the town faded into the background, replaced by the howling wind and the bitter cold. Mary huddled in the doorway, her body trembling uncontrollably. She didn't know what would happen to her, but she couldn't keep going. She could only hope that someone would find her before it was too late.

The freezing cold seeped deeper into her bones, and she felt a creeping numbness spreading through her limbs. She knew the signs of hypothermia and worried that she wouldn't last much longer out in the open. The exhaustion was too great, and she couldn't bring herself to move anymore. Every breath she took felt like shards of ice cutting into her lungs.

Her vision blurred, and she became aware of a figure standing in front of her. She blinked, trying to focus, but the person remained a shadowy blur. For a fleeting moment, she thought it might be Mr Everly, come to take her back, to offer her the warmth and shelter she so desperately needed.

"Are you okay?" The voice sounded distant, muffled by the wind and her failing senses. She tried to respond, to reach out, but her strength had left her.

The figure knelt beside her, and she felt a hand on her shoulder, gently shaking her. "Miss, can you hear me?"

Mary's eyes fluttered, the world around her darkening. She wanted to answer, to grasp onto this glimmer of hope, but her body refused to obey. The cold had taken hold, and she felt herself slipping away, the edges of her vision closing in.

The last thing she heard was the concerned voice trying to reach her, the words fading into the void. Her body went limp, and everything went black.

Chapter Eighteen

Mary awoke hours later, disoriented and surrounded by unfamiliar warmth. She blinked against the dim light, her senses slowly returning. The room around her was unlike any she had seen before: elegant, with soft cream-coloured walls and rich, dark wood furniture. Heavy drapes framed a large window, which was covered with frost on the outside. A small, crackling fire in the corner provided a comforting glow, casting flickering shadows across a plush armchair and a neatly made bed.

Mary's heart raced with panic as she tried to make sense of her surroundings. How had she gotten here? Was she safe? She sat up quickly, the soft blankets slipping off her shoulders, and swung her legs over the side of the bed. She took a moment to gather her bearings, her fingers trembling as she gripped the edge of the mattress.

The room was beautifully furnished, with a vanity table topped with delicate glass bottles and a small vase of dried flowers. The air smelled faintly of lavender, and the warmth from the fire seeped into her bones, chasing away the chill that had settled deep within her.

Mary stood and made her way to the window, hoping to recognise something outside. She pulled back the heavy drapes, but it was too dark to see much beyond the frosted glass. The street below was unfamiliar, the faint outline of buildings barely visible in the night.

Her mind raced with questions. Who had brought her here? Why had they taken her in? Her heart pounded in her chest as she turned away from the window, the feeling of vulnerability washing over her. She had to find out where she was and if she was truly safe.

As she stood there, the door creaked open, and a figure stepped into the room. Mary's breath caught in her throat as she saw who it was.

"John?" she whispered, her voice a mix of disbelief and relief.

John Bradshaw stood in the doorway, his handsome face illuminated by the soft glow of the fire. He looked much the same as she remembered: tall and lean, with a strong jawline and kind, dark eyes that seemed to pierce through the dim light. His hair was slightly tousled, and he wore a warm, inviting smile that made Mary's heart flutter.

"Mary," he said gently, stepping closer. "You're awake. How are you feeling?"

Tears of relief welled up in Mary's eyes as she took in the sight of him. "John, I... I don't understand. How did I get here?"

John moved to her side, his presence comforting and reassuring. "I found you last night, passed out in the snow. You were freezing, Mary. I couldn't leave you there, so I brought you here to my home."

Mary's mind raced, trying to piece together the events of the night before. She remembered the cold, the fear, and the darkness closing in. "You saved me," she whispered, her voice trembling.

John nodded, his expression serious. "You were in a bad way. I'm just glad I found you in time."

She looked up at him, her heart swelling with gratitude. "Thank you, John. I don't know what would have happened if you hadn't..."

He placed a gentle hand on her shoulder, his touch warm and comforting. "You don't need to thank me. I couldn't just leave you out there. You're safe now."

Mary felt a rush of emotions: relief, gratitude, and something deeper, a sense of connection she hadn't felt in a long time. She gazed at John, taking in his handsome features, the kindness in his eyes.

Mary realised she was still dressed in her damp, cold clothes as she tore her gaze away from John. She shivered, the fabric clinging uncomfortably to her skin. John noticed her discomfort. "I'm sorry, Mary. I didn't want to change you without your permission, and my housekeeper had left for the night. I hope you understand."

She nodded, cheeks flushed. "Thank you, John. I appreciate that."

He smiled warmly. "I have a few spare dresses you can wear. They're my sister's. She left them here the last time she visited.

They're much nicer than anything I have to offer otherwise."

Mary's eyes widened with surprise. "Thank you, John. That's very kind of you."

John retrieved a dress from a nearby wardrobe and handed it to her. It was a beautiful garment, made of soft, flowing fabric in a delicate shade of blue. Mary ran her fingers over the material, marvelling at its quality.

"I'll give you some privacy to change," John said, stepping out of the room. "If you need anything, just call. My housekeeper has just arrived as well."

Mary nodded, grateful for his thoughtfulness. She began to undress, her fingers clumsy with cold and exhaustion. As she peeled off her damp clothes, she felt a wave of relief. She slipped into the dress, the fabric feeling soft and warm against her skin.

As she reached for the fresh stockings John had provided, a sudden dizziness overcame her. The room spun around her, and she struggled to stay upright. She took a deep breath, trying to steady herself, but the dizziness intensified. She stumbled, knocking into the bed, and felt herself falling.

The noise of her fall must have been loud, because within seconds, John and a housekeeper rushed into the room. John's eyes widened in alarm as he saw Mary collapsed on the floor, her face pale and her breathing shallow.

"Mary!" he exclaimed, kneeling beside her. "Are you okay?"

The housekeeper, a middle-aged woman with a kind face, quickly assessed the situation. "We need to get her back into bed," she said firmly. "She's still weak and needs rest."

John nodded, gently lifting Mary and placing her back on the bed. Mary's head swam, but she was aware of their concerned faces hovering above her.

"Thank you," she managed to whisper, her voice faint.

The housekeeper smiled reassuringly. "Don't worry, dear. You're safe here. Just rest."

John's expression was filled with concern and determination. "We'll take care of you, Mary. You need to regain your strength."

Mary lay back in the bed, her body still trembling from the cold and the shock of the past day. The housekeeper, a woman with a gentle French accent and a motherly face, leaned over her, brushing a stray lock of hair from her forehead.

"You can stay here while you recover, dear," the housekeeper said softly. "My name is Elodie. I will be your chaperone and take care of you."

Mary felt a wave of relief wash over her. "Thank you, Elodie. I don't want to be a burden."

Elodie smiled warmly. "Nonsense, ma chère. You are not a burden. You need rest and care, and that is what you will get here."

Mary looked at John, who was standing by the bedside, his expression filled with concern. "What's wrong with me?" she asked, her voice barely above a whisper.

John knelt down beside her, taking her hand in his. "You might have hypothermia from being out in the cold for so long. Your body needs to warm up and recover. It's important that you rest and allow yourself to heal."

Mary struggled with the idea of staying in bed and being looked after. She had always been independent, working hard to support herself. The thought of being a burden weighed heavily on her mind. "I'm not used to being taken care of," she admitted, her eyes filling with tears. "I don't want to impose."

John squeezed her hand gently. "You're not imposing, Mary. We want to help you. Please, let us take care of you."

Elodie nodded in agreement, her eyes kind and reassuring. "You must rest, dear. Your health is the most important thing right now. We will take care of everything else."

Mary looked between John and Elodie, feeling a deep sense of gratitude. She knew she was in good hands, and their kindness was overwhelming. "Thank you," she whispered, her voice choked with emotion.

John stood up, giving her a reassuring smile. "I'll leave you to rest now. If you need anything, Elodie will be right here."

Mary nodded, her eyelids growing heavy with exhaustion. "Thank you, John. For everything."

John looked at her with a tenderness that made her heart ache. "You're welcome, Mary. Get some rest. We'll talk more when you're feeling better."

With that, John left the room, closing the door softly behind him. Elodie pulled a chair up to the bedside and sat down, her presence comforting and steady. "Rest now, ma chère. I will be here if you need anything."

Mary's eyes fluttered then closed, the warmth of the bed and the gentle crackling of the fire lulling her into a deep sleep. She felt safe, surrounded by the kindness of John and his housekeeper who had become her protectors. As she drifted off, she whispered a silent prayer of gratitude, knowing that she was not alone in this world after all.

***

Mary awoke in the middle of the night, the room around her dimly lit by the dying embers of the fire. She felt disoriented at first, but then the memories of the day flooded back. The warmth and comfort of the bed contrasted sharply with the cold she had endured outside. She looked around and noticed that Elodie was no longer sitting by her bedside.

She must have slept for hours, and the house was quiet. The chill in the air seeped through the blankets, so Mary bundled up in the thick covers and carefully slipped out of bed. Her feet touched the cold floor, and she shivered. She needed to find out where Elodie had gone, and perhaps get a glass of water.

Mary slowly opened the door to the hallway, the hinges creaking softly. The corridor was dimly lit by a few wall sconces, casting long shadows that danced on the walls. She tiptoed down the hall, her ears straining to catch any sound. As she approached the end of the hallway, she heard voices coming from a nearby room.

She hesitated, recognizing the voices. It was John and Elodie. She moved closer, careful to stay hidden, and listened.

"I'm so worried about her, Elodie," John was saying, his voice filled with concern. "She was in such a bad state when I found her. I can't believe she had to go through that alone."

Elodie's voice was gentle and reassuring. "She is safe now, John. You did the right thing bringing her here. She just needs time to recover."

John sighed deeply. "I know, but I can't help but feel responsible. I should have been there for her sooner. Seeing her like that... it broke my heart."

Mary's heart skipped a beat at his words. She leaned in closer, wanting to hear more.

"She is a strong young woman," Elodie said. "But even the strongest need help sometimes. And I think she is very lucky to have you looking out for her."

John's voice softened. "I've missed her, Elodie. Seeing her again, even under these circumstances, it... it makes me happy. I'm just glad she's safe now."

Mary felt a rush of relief and a spark of hope ignite within her. John cared for her deeply; she could hear it in his voice. The fear and uncertainty that had plagued her began to melt away, replaced by the warmth of knowing she wasn't alone. Maybe, just maybe, John's feelings for her were more than just concern for a friend.

She stepped back, her heart racing with this newfound hope. She quietly made her way back to the room, slipping under the covers and feeling the cold of the night retreat. As she lay there, the soft murmurs of their conversation fading into the background, Mary allowed herself to dream of a future that was brighter, filled with the possibility of love and happiness.

For the first time in a long while, she felt truly safe and cared for. With a contented sigh, she closed her eyes, letting the warmth of the bed and the hope in her heart lull her back to sleep.

Chapter Nineteen

The next morning, Mary awoke to the soft light of dawn filtering through the heavy drapes. The room, now warmer from the rekindled fire, felt like a sanctuary. She stretched, feeling the stiffness in her limbs begin to ease, and a gentle knock at the door caught her attention.

"Good morning, Mary," Elodie's kind voice greeted her as she entered the room, carrying a fresh set of clothes and a warm smile. "How are you feeling today?"

"Better, thank you," Mary replied, her voice still a bit raspy from the cold.

Elodie helped Mary to her feet and guided her to the adjoining room where a warm bath awaited. The steam rose gently from the water, and Mary felt a deep sense of relief as she sank into the tub, the warmth soothing her tired muscles.

"I'll be right here if you need anything," Elodie said, placing a towel and fresh clothes within reach. "Take your time."

After the bath, Mary felt rejuvenated. Elodie helped her dress in a soft, comfortable dress, similar to the one she had worn the night before. The fabric felt luxurious against her skin, and she couldn't help but feel a bit self-conscious about wearing something so fine.

Once dressed, Mary followed Elodie to the dining room, where a simple but inviting breakfast was laid out on the table. John was already seated, his face lighting up with a warm smile as he saw her enter.

"Good morning, Mary. I hope you slept well," he said, standing to pull out a chair for her.

"Good morning, John. I did, thank you," Mary replied, taking her seat.

Elodie joined them at the table, and Mary couldn't help but notice how John treated her more like a friend than a housekeeper. The three of them chatted amicably, and Mary felt a sense of normalcy and comfort she hadn't experienced in a long time.

John laughed at something Elodie said, and Mary's curiosity got the better of her.

"You seem very close," she observed, looking between them.

John nodded, a fond smile on his face. "Elodie is an old friend of my mother's. When her husband passed away, she came to work for me. She's more like family than anything else."

Elodie smiled warmly. "Yes, and I live just a few minutes away. John has been a great help to me as well. We look out for each other."

Mary found herself admiring the easy rapport between them. It was clear that there was deep mutual respect and affection. The breakfast, though simple, was delicious: warm bread with butter and jam, fresh eggs, and hot tea. Mary savoured each bite, feeling nourished and cared for.

As they ate, Mary couldn't help but steal glances at John. His handsome features were softened by the morning light, and his laughter was infectious. He seemed so different from the stern, reserved figure she had once known in the parish. There was a gentleness and warmth about him that she found incredibly endearing.

"Mary," John said, interrupting her thoughts, "I'm glad you're feeling better. If there's anything you need or if you feel unwell, please let us know."

Mary nodded, her heart swelling with gratitude. "Thank you, John. I can't thank you enough for everything you've done."

John smiled, his eyes meeting hers with a sincerity that made her heart flutter. "You don't need to thank me, Mary. I'm just glad you're here and safe."

The rest of the breakfast passed in a comfortable silence, filled with the sounds of clinking cutlery and the occasional soft laughter. Mary felt a deep sense of contentment, surrounded by the kindness of John and Elodie.

As the meal concluded, John rose from his seat. "I have some errands to run this morning, but Elodie will be here if you need anything. Please, make yourself at home."

Mary nodded, feeling a mix of gratitude and admiration. "Thank you, John."

As John left the room, Mary turned to Elodie. "You're very lucky to have each other."

Elodie's eyes twinkled with warmth. "We are, indeed. Now, let's get you settled and comfortable. You need to rest."

***

That afternoon, John returned from his errands and found Mary sitting by the fire, staring into the dancing flames. He entered the room quietly, his presence comforting.

"Mary," he said gently, "you should be recovering in bed."

Mary looked up, a faint smile on her lips. "I know, John, but I hate sitting still. Elodie wouldn't let me help with the housekeeping, and it's all I know how to do."

John chuckled softly, pulling up a chair beside her. "Elodie is right; you need to rest.

Perhaps talking might help keep your mind off things."

Mary nodded, appreciating his thoughtfulness. John settled into the chair, and Elodie pottered about the room, tidying up and occasionally glancing over with a motherly smile.

"Tell me about your friends, Mary," John said, leaning forward slightly. "Do you miss them?"

Mary's eyes softened with sadness. "I do. Lizzie and Annie were like sisters to me. We worked together, laughed together, and shared our burdens. Then there were my old friends from the orphanage. We always looked out for each other."

John listened intently, his expression compassionate. "It sounds like they meant a great deal to you."

"They did," Mary replied, her voice tinged with longing. "I wish I could see them again, especially Annie. After what happened, I don't think I'll be welcomed back at the Everly townhouse."

John's brow furrowed. "I'm sorry for what you went through, Mary. It wasn't fair, and you deserve better."

Mary sighed, staring into the fire. "Thank you, John. It's just hard to accept that I've lost everything. I can't go back to the place I called home, and I don't know what to do next."

John reached out, gently taking her hand. "Perhaps, when you're feeling better, you could visit Lizzie and Annie. You don't have to go back to work there, but seeing them might bring some comfort."

Mary looked at him, a glimmer of hope in her eyes. "I'd like that, but I'm afraid they might not want to see me after everything that's happened."

John squeezed her hand reassuringly. "True friends will understand and welcome you back, no matter the circumstances. If they care about you as much as you care about them, they'll be glad to see you."

Mary's eyes filled with tears, but this time they were tears of gratitude. "I hope you're right, John. I miss them so much."

John smiled warmly. "I am right, Mary. You have friends here too. Elodie and I are here for you."

Elodie, who had been listening quietly, nodded in agreement. "Absolutely, dear. You are always welcome here."

Mary felt a warmth spread through her heart, melting away some of the fear and uncertainty. "Thank you, both of you. Your kindness means more to me than I can say."

They spent the rest of the afternoon talking, the conversation flowing easily as they shared stories and memories. John's presence was a balm to Mary's troubled heart, and she found herself feeling lighter, more hopeful. The fire crackled softly, casting a warm glow over the room, and for the first time in weeks, Mary felt a sense of peace.

Chapter Twenty

A few days passed, and Mary began to settle into a comfortable routine at John's home. Each morning, she woke to the smell of fresh bread and the sound of Elodie humming softly in the kitchen. The warmth of the house and the kindness of her hosts brought a sense of stability that she had sorely missed.

During breakfast, Mary hesitated before speaking. She had been thinking about it for a while and finally decided to bring it up. "John, Elodie, I've been feeling much better these past few days. I think it's time I start looking for a job. Do either of you have any recommendations?"

John and Elodie exchanged glances, their expressions quickly shifting from surprise to concern.

"Mary, you really should be focusing on your recovery," John said gently. "There's no need to rush into finding work."

Elodie nodded in agreement. "You've been through a lot, dear. Your health is the most important thing right now."

Mary sighed, feeling a bit frustrated. "I appreciate your concern, truly, but I don't want to overstay my welcome. I need to start taking care of myself, and that means finding work."

John's eyes softened with understanding, but he remained firm. "You are not overstaying your welcome, Mary. You can stay here as long as you need. Right now, you should focus on getting better."

Elodie placed a comforting hand on Mary's arm. "Listen to John, dear. You've been through so much, and your body needs time to heal. There will be plenty of time to think about work later."

Mary looked between the two of them, her heart swelling with gratitude. "Thank you, both of you. I just don't want to be a burden."

John smiled warmly. "You are not a burden, Mary. You're a friend, and we care about you. Your well-being is our priority."

Elodie nodded, her eyes filled with kindness. "Indeed. We want you to feel at home here. Take the time you need to recover fully. The world can wait."

Mary felt tears prick at the corners of her eyes, touched by their unwavering support. "I'll try not to push myself too hard."

They finished their breakfast, and Elodie poured tea, the fragrant steam rising from the delicate porcelain cups. Mary sipped her tea, trying to focus on the warmth and comfort of the moment, but her mind kept wandering. How long until their hospitality ran out? Or something else bad happened? It seemed that whenever she began to get too comfortable, things went wrong.

After they finished eating, Mary insisted on helping Elodie with the dishes. Despite her protests, Elodie finally relented with a smile, and the two of them moved to the kitchen. As they worked, John excused himself and went to his study, leaving the women to their tasks.

Mary began washing the dishes, the warm water soothing her hands. Elodie dried and put them away, her movements graceful and efficient. The silence between them was comfortable, punctuated only by the clinking of dishes and the splash of water.

"John has been so kind to me," Mary said after a while, her voice thoughtful. "I don't know how I'll ever repay him."

Elodie glanced at her, a knowing smile playing on her lips. "John has always been kind-hearted. He has a way of making people feel valued and cared for."

Mary nodded, her thoughts drifting to John's gentle demeanour and the warmth in his eyes. "He's been more than kind. He saved me. I don't know what I would have done without him."

Elodie set a dish down and turned to face Mary, her expression gentle but probing. "You care for him deeply, don't you?"

Mary felt her cheeks flush, and she looked down at the soapy water. "I do. He's... he's everything I've ever hoped for in a friend."

Elodie's smile widened, her eyes twinkling. "It's more than friendship, isn't it?"

Mary's heart skipped a beat, and she took a deep breath. "Yes, it is. I've never felt this way about anyone before. I'm afraid to hope for too much. It seems like whenever I get too comfortable, things go wrong."

Elodie reached out and placed a comforting hand on Mary's arm. "Life has a way of testing us, but it's also full of unexpected blessings. John cares for you too, Mary. I see it in the way he looks at you, the way he talks about you."

Mary looked up, hope flickering in her eyes. "Do you really think so?"

Elodie nodded, her expression earnest. "I do. Give it time, ma chere. Allow yourself to heal and let things unfold naturally. Trust in the kindness you see in John, and trust in yourself."

Mary sighed, feeling the weight of Elodie's words sink in. "It's just hard to let go of the fear. I've been hurt so many times before, and I don't know if I can bear it happening again."

Elodie squeezed her arm gently. "I understand, Mary. Sometimes, the greatest rewards come from taking the greatest risks. You are stronger than you know, and you deserve to be happy."

Mary nodded, a mixture of hope and apprehension swirling within her. "Your words mean a lot to me."

They continued chatting as they finished the last of the dishes. Elodie shared stories of her past, her gentle French accent adding a musical lilt to her words. Mary found herself laughing and feeling more at ease, the warmth of the kitchen and Elodie's companionship soothing her troubled heart.

Just as they were putting the last dish away, they heard footsteps approaching. Mary quickly dried her hands and tried to compose herself. Elodie gave her a knowing look and a reassuring smile as John entered the kitchen.

"Is everything all right in here?" John asked, his eyes scanning the room before settling on Mary.

"Everything's fine," Mary replied, her voice steady. "We were just finishing up."

John smiled, a look of relief on his face. "Good. I was thinking we could have a chat, Mary, if you're up for it."

Mary glanced at Elodie, who nodded encouragingly. "Of course, John," she said, following him into the sitting room.

They sat by the fire, the warm glow casting comforting shadows around them. John leaned forward, his expression earnest. "Mary, I've been wanting to talk to you about something. I know you've been through a lot, and I want to make sure you're all right."

Mary took a deep breath, feeling the weight of his concern. "Thank you, John. I appreciate your kindness more than I can say. It's just..."

"What is it?" John asked gently.

Mary hesitated, choosing her words carefully. "I've been so afraid to settle down, to trust in the stability and kindness of others. It feels like whenever I start to get comfortable, something bad happens. I don't want to be a burden to you or to outstay my welcome."

John's eyes softened with understanding. "You're not a burden, Mary. I want you to feel safe and welcome here. Take all the time you need to heal. There's no rush."

Mary nodded, her heart aching with unspoken feelings. She wanted to tell him how much she admired him, how deeply she cared for him, but she held back at the last second. Instead, she said, "It's just hard to let go of the fear. I've lost so much already."

John reached out and took her hand, his touch warm and reassuring. "I understand, Mary. I'm here for you. You don't have to face anything alone."

Tears welled up in Mary's eyes, and she squeezed his hand gratefully.

They sat in comfortable silence for a moment, the crackling of the fire the only sound in the room. Mary felt a sense of peace settling over her, knowing she had found a true friend in John.

Elodie's gentle footsteps approached, and she peeked into the room. Seeing them together, she smiled warmly. "Tea is ready, if you'd like some," Elodie said, her voice soft and inviting.

John smiled and released Mary's hand, standing up. "That sounds lovely."

Mary followed him to the kitchen, feeling a mixture of relief and uncertainty. She had managed to share some of her fears without revealing her deepest feelings, and for now, that was enough. They sat down together at the table, Elodie pouring the tea with her usual grace.

As they sipped their tea, the atmosphere was filled with a comfortable silence, occasionally broken by light conversation. Elodie shared more stories from her past, and John and Mary listened, both finding comfort in her gentle voice and kind demeanour.

Mary glanced at John from time to time, her heart swelling with admiration and gratitude. She was beginning to feel that, perhaps, this time, things might not go wrong. With Elodie's wisdom and John's steadfast support, she dared to hope for a future where she could truly belong.

After tea, John excused himself to return to his study, leaving Mary and Elodie to tidy up the kitchen. As they worked, Elodie leaned in and whispered, "You did well, Mary. Give it time, and things will become clearer."

Mary nodded, feeling a surge of gratitude for Elodie's understanding and support. "Do you think so? Honestly, I don't know what I would do without you and John."

She smiled. "Things will turn out just fine. I know it."

Chapter Twenty-One

The week before Christmas arrived with a flurry of activity and excitement. John watched as Elodie and Mary bustled about, their laughter filling the house with warmth. The air was filled with the scent of pine and baking spices, and the sound of Christmas carols played softly in the background.

"John, could you help me with this garland?" Mary called from the living room, her cheeks flushed with the warmth from the fire.

"Of course," John replied, walking over to where she stood. He took one end of the garland and began to drape it across the mantle, carefully arranging the greenery so it hung just right. Elodie joined them, humming a tune as she worked on the other side of the room, hanging ornaments on the tree.

"This place is going to look wonderful," Elodie said, stepping back to admire their handiwork. "It feels like Christmas already."

Mary smiled, her eyes shining with happiness. "This will be my first real Christmas in years. I've spent so many holidays alone, or working, or just trying to survive. This year, it feels like I have a family again."

John felt a warmth spread through his chest at her words. He looked at Mary, seeing the joy in her expression, and felt a surge of protectiveness and affection. "We are your family, Mary; we're so glad you're here with us."

Mary's smile widened, and she continued to hang the decorations with renewed enthusiasm. "I can't help but wonder how my father and friends are doing, though. I hope they're all right."

John stepped closer, gently placing a hand on her shoulder. "Try not to think about that now. Focus on this moment, and the joy of being here together."

Mary nodded, her expression softening. "You're right, John. This is where I need to be."

As they continued to decorate, John couldn't help but feel a deep sense of contentment. He watched Mary and Elodie laugh and chat, their voices blending harmoniously with the music. The tree sparkled with lights and ornaments, and the room glowed with the warmth of the season.

At one point, Mary was attempting to hang some tinsel, and John noticed she was getting bits of it in her hair. He chuckled softly, stepping forward to help her. "Hold still, Mary. You've got tinsel everywhere."

She laughed, standing still as John gently picked the tinsel from her hair. His fingers brushed against her soft locks, and he felt a familiar warmth spread through him. "There," he said, smiling down at her. "All sorted."

Mary looked up at him, her eyes shining and cheeks flushed. "Oh, thank you."

John felt his heart swell with affection. "You're welcome, Mary. I'm just glad we can share this time together."

John knew, deep in his heart, that he loved Mary. He had watched her transform from a frightened, cold girl at his doorstep to a vibrant, joyful woman who filled his home with laughter and warmth.

As they decorated the house together, he couldn't help but think about the secret he was keeping—a special surprise he hoped to reveal on Christmas. He believed it would bring her the happiness she deserved.

They finished decorating the tree, the garland, and the rest of the house, stepping back to admire their work. The home looked magical, every corner filled with the spirit of the season. John felt a profound sense of contentment.

Elodie clapped her hands together, a satisfied smile on her face. "It looks beautiful. This will be a Christmas to remember."

The moment lingered. John finally broke the silence with a warm smile. "I hope to see both of you at church tomorrow for the Sunday service. It's the last one before Christmas, and it would mean a lot to me to have you there."

Mary's face lit up with excitement. "I wouldn't miss it for anything, John."

Elodie nodded in agreement. "Of course, John. We'll be there."

The rest of the evening passed in a comfortable, festive mood. They shared stories, laughed, and enjoyed the warmth of the fire. John couldn't help but feel a sense of anticipation, knowing that the surprise he had planned would make this Christmas unforgettable for Mary.

As they all retired for the night, John found himself lingering in the living room, staring at the twinkling lights on the tree. He hoped with all his heart that Mary would love the surprise and that it would bring them even closer together.

***

The next morning, John was up early, preparing for the day. He could hear Elodie and Mary moving about the house, getting ready for church. The sun was just starting to rise, casting a soft glow over the freshly fallen snow outside.

When they were all ready, John led the way to the small church down the street. The walk was peaceful, the crisp air filled with the promise of the season. As they approached the church, the sound of bells ringing welcomed them.

Inside, the church was beautifully decorated with greenery and candles, the scent of pine and beeswax filling the air. The congregation was already gathering, their faces bright with anticipation for the upcoming holiday.

Mary and Elodie found a pew near the front, settling in as the service began. The familiar hymns and readings filled the air, and John felt a deep sense of peace. He glanced at Mary from across the church, who was singing along with the carols, her face radiant with joy. It warmed his heart to see her so happy.

As the carols came to a close, John stepped up to the pulpit, his heart full as he prepared to lead the sermon. He looked out at the congregation, his gaze lingering on Mary for a moment longer before he began to speak.

"Good morning, everyone," he greeted, his voice steady and warm. "As we gather here today, just a week before Christmas, I want us to reflect on the true meaning of this season. It's a time for love, for kindness, and for being with those we care about. It's a time to open our hearts and to let the light of Christ shine through us."

He saw Mary smiling, her eyes shining with understanding and warmth. It gave him the strength to continue, his words flowing with ease.

"Christmas is not just about the decorations, the gifts, or the feasts. It is about the love we share and the hope we bring to each other's lives. It is a reminder that, no matter how dark the world may seem, there is always light. That light comes from the love we give and receive."

John paused, letting his words sink in. He looked at Mary again, feeling a deep connection as he continued. "In this season of giving, let us remember those who may feel alone, those who are in need of kindness. Let us open our hearts and homes to them, showing them that they are not forgotten. For it is through these acts of love that we truly celebrate the spirit of Christmas."

As he finished his sermon, John felt a wave of warmth and gratitude from the congregation. He led them in a final prayer, then stepped down from the pulpit, feeling a sense of fulfilment and peace.

After the service, John made his way through the crowd, greeting parishioners and exchanging warm wishes. He finally reached Mary and Elodie, who were waiting for him near the door.

"That was a beautiful sermon, John," Mary said, her eyes sparkling with sincerity.

"I think so too," he replied, smiling warmly. "I'm glad you enjoyed it."

Elodie nodded in agreement. "It was indeed moving, John. You spoke straight to the heart."

They began their walk home, the crisp winter air invigorating and fresh. Mary walked beside John, her steps light and her expression filled with excitement.

"I feel like this is the first Christmas I've truly been able to enjoy," Mary said, her voice filled with wonder. "Thank you both for making it so special."

John felt a surge of happiness at her words. "We're happy to have you with us. It's been wonderful seeing you so happy and at ease."

Mary smiled up at him, her face radiant. "I never thought I could feel this way again. You've given me so much to be thankful for."

John's heart swelled with emotion. He was overjoyed to see Mary finally allowing herself to be happy, to embrace the warmth and love that surrounded her. "You have given us so much as well, Mary. Your presence has brought joy to our home."

For a moment, John felt an overwhelming urge to kiss her, to show her just how much she meant to him. He knew it would be improper, given the circumstances. Instead, he smiled warmly and walked beside her as they made their way back home.

When they arrived, Elodie immediately set about making tea, while John watched Mary adjust some decorations on the tree. She stood on tiptoe, carefully placing an ornament that had shifted out of place. Her concentration was intense, and a soft smile played on her lips.

John approached her, his voice gentle. "You have a knack for making everything look perfect."

Mary turned to him, her eyes softening. "I'll always be a housekeeper at heart, I suppose. I just want everything to be as beautiful as it feels."

She hesitated for a moment, then sighed. "I wish my father was here. Not because I miss him, but because I think he'd see what a real family looks like. I stopped feeling guilty over what happened a long time ago. He wasn't a good father, and I've come to terms with that."

John stepped closer, his gaze steady and reassuring. "You have nothing to feel guilty about, Mary. You've shown so much strength and courage. You deserve to be happy, surrounded by people who care for you."

Mary looked at him, a mix of gratitude and relief in her eyes. "It *is* good to be here. I promise, I don't mean to complain."

Elodie entered the room with a tray of tea, her presence as comforting as ever. "I hope I'm not interrupting," she said with a smile, setting the tray down on a small table.

"Not at all, Elodie," John replied, taking a seat beside Mary. "We were just having a chat."

Elodie poured the tea, her movements graceful and practiced. She handed a cup to Mary, then one to John. "Here you go, dears. Nothing like a warm cup of tea on a chilly day."

Mary took the cup, savouring the warmth. "This is perfect."

They sat together, the room filled with a sense of peace and camaraderie. John watched Mary as she sipped her tea, her face reflecting a quiet contentment. He felt a deep sense of gratitude for these moments, for the chance to be part of her journey toward healing and happiness.

As they sat in comfortable silence, John couldn't help but think about the surprise he had planned for Christmas. He hoped it would show Mary just how much she meant to him, and how deeply he cared for her. For now, he was content to simply be in her presence, to share these simple, beautiful moments together.

Chapter Twenty-Two

On Christmas morning, Mary woke with a sense of anticipation and joy she hadn't felt in years. The house was filled with the delicious aroma of breakfast being cooked by Elodie. As she got dressed, she could hear the gentle hum of conversation and the occasional burst of laughter coming from the kitchen.

She joined John and Elodie downstairs, the warmth of the kitchen and the sight of their smiling faces making her heart swell. Elodie had prepared a feast: scrambled eggs, crispy bacon, fresh pastries, and a pot of tea that seemed to warm the soul.

"Merry Christmas!" Mary greeted them, taking her seat at the table.

"Merry Christmas, Mary!" Elodie and John echoed.

They sat together, enjoying the hearty breakfast. The food was delicious, as always, but Elodie had made it even better with crisp bacon from the butcher's and fresh butter.

After breakfast, they moved to the sitting room, where the fire crackled cheerfully, and the Christmas tree sparkled with lights and ornaments. They settled around the fire, ready to exchange gifts. Mary had been nervous about her presents; she didn't have much money, but she had put a lot of thought into what she could give.

She handed Elodie a neatly wrapped package. "This is for you, Elodie. Merry Christmas."

Elodie opened the gift carefully, revealing a beautifully embroidered handkerchief. Mary had spent hours stitching the delicate flowers and patterns. "Oh, Mary, this is lovely!" Elodie exclaimed, her eyes shining with gratitude. "You have such a talent. Thank you so much."

Mary smiled, feeling a warmth spread through her heart. "I'm glad you like it."

Next, she handed John a small parcel. "*This* is for you, John."

John unwrapped the package to find a simple yet elegant leather bookmark. Mary had etched his initials into it, adding a personal touch. John's eyes softened as he looked at it. "This is wonderful, Mary. Thank you. I'll think of you every time I use it."

Mary felt her cheeks flush with happiness.

They exchanged a few more gifts, the room filled with laughter and warmth. Mary cherished each moment, grateful for the kindness and love that surrounded her.

As the gift-giving came to a close, John stood up, a different kind of smile on his face. "I have one more gift," he said, his voice filled with emotion. He reached into his pocket and pulled out a small box.

Mary's heart began to race as he approached her, the box held carefully in his hands. He knelt down in front of her, opening the box to reveal a delicate ring. The sight of it took Mary's breath away.

"Mary," John began, his voice steady but filled with emotion. "From the moment I met you, you've brought light into my life. You are kind, brave, and strong. I can't imagine my future without you in it."

Tears welled up in Mary's eyes as she listened to his heartfelt words. She felt a surge of love and hope, her heart pounding in her chest.

"Will you do me the honour of becoming my wife?" John asked, his eyes never leaving hers. "Will you marry me, Mary?"

Mary's heart swelled with emotion, but a wave of doubt washed over her. "John, I... I'm not sure I'm good enough to be a vicar's wife. What if I can't meet the expectations?"

John's eyes softened with understanding. He took her hands in his, his touch warm and reassuring. "Mary, you are more than good enough. You are kind, compassionate, and strong. I love you for who you are, not for who you think you need to be."

Mary looked into his eyes, seeing the sincerity and love there. Her doubts began to melt away. "Do you really mean that, John?"

"With all my heart," he replied, his voice filled with conviction. "You complete me, Mary. I want to spend the rest of my life with you."

Overwhelmed with love and certainty, Mary nodded, tears spilling down her cheeks. "Yes, John. Yes, I will marry you."

John's face lit up with joy. He gently wiped away her tears before leaning in to kiss her. It was a tender, sweet kiss, filled with the promise of a future together.

Elodie clapped her hands, tears of happiness in her eyes. "Oh, this is wonderful! Congratulations, both of you!"

John smiled at Elodie before turning back to Mary. He opened the small box, revealing a delicate ring. It was a simple yet elegant band of gold, set with a small, sparkling diamond in the centre, flanked by two tiny sapphires. It was perfect, timeless, and beautiful—much like their love.

He slipped the ring onto Mary's finger, and she admired how it caught the light, symbolizing their shared commitment and the bright future ahead.

"It's beautiful," Mary whispered, her voice filled with awe.

John kissed her hand gently. "Just like you."

They embraced again, their hearts full of love and hope. Elodie watched them with a beaming smile, clearly overjoyed for the couple.

"This is truly a Christmas miracle," Elodie said, her voice trembling. "I'm so happy for both of you. You deserve all the happiness in the world."

Mary looked around the room, feeling an overwhelming sense of gratitude and love. She had found a family, a home, and a future filled with promise. This Christmas was the beginning of a new chapter in her life, one that she couldn't wait to embark on with John by her side.

As they sat together by the fire, their hands intertwined, Mary felt a deep sense of peace and contentment. She knew that, no matter what challenges lay ahead, they would face them together, their love guiding them through.

This was the Christmas she had always dreamed of, filled with love, joy, and the promise of a bright future. This was her Christmas miracle. And as she looked into John's eyes, she knew that this was only the beginning of a beautiful journey together.

Printed in Great Britain
by Amazon